ip '73 4.95

The Revolutionary

The Revolutionary

a novel by
HANS KONINGSBERGER

FARRAR, STRAUS AND GIROUX ■ NEW YORK

All roads led into a morass, in my days.
Words gave us away to the executioner.
There was little I could do. Yet our rulers
would have been happier without me, I hoped.
Thus passed the time
allotted to me on this earth.

> FROM "For those born after us,"
> by Bertolt Brecht

The Revolutionary

I

He was lying on a straw mattress in an attic room of the massive building.

It had been one of the first modern apartment houses put up in that town, but before the paint was dry it had already begun deteriorating into the semi-tenement it was now, filled with clerks of the lowest ranks, struggling salesmen, notaries, assistant lecturers at the Latin schools, and their large and wan families. The attic room was one of a row intended by the builders for maids' quarters, but as there were very few servants, these rooms were rented out separately.

Lifting his head he could see the sky, an uninterrupted field of grey reflecting the fading light of the autumn day. His movements were slow and painful, for his right leg was broken and had been splinted and bandaged with more love than experience by a fellow student of his, a man in third-year medical school.

3

It must be past six, he thought, I'll have to get over to the window.

It would not really be that difficult, but it took him time to start since he could anticipate precisely the kind of pain it was going to cause. He sat up on his bed and then he edged toward the chair beside it. He hoisted himself upright, and hopped to his window, pushing the chair along as a support. There was a ledge along the wall and once he had scrambled up on that and lifted his splinted leg up in front of him, he was fairly comfortable. He pushed the sloping window open and leaned out sideways. Because of the gutter he could see only the part of the street beyond the middle, and the sidewalk and low houses opposite.

There was no one in sight.

A leaden light seemed to descend from the sky and weigh on the town. It was so still, so endlessly melancholy, he thought, that just from observing this small section of one street it should be possible to divine history, to know that here was a street in the very heart of Europe, far from what he imagined to be sunnier and lighter countries touched by the sea. So many tired steps must have been set here, he thought, it is a miracle that this street of mine hasn't been pushed down below the surface of the earth.

There were two street lamps, one on each corner, recently converted from gas to electricity—an event hailed by *The People*, the government newspaper, as the true ringing in, if a couple of years late, of the twentieth century. He could see them both, black lamp posts decorated with ghoulish cast-iron leaves shaped like no leaf that ever grew. Just then they went on (he imagined he heard the plop sound the old gaslights used to make) and shone out small circles of yellow light at each street end. That meant it was seven o'clock exactly: the appointed hour.

At that moment one single shot was heard, from far away, followed after a few seconds by another. There was muted shouting; then again silence.

Not a window opened, no one stirred; the emptiness of the street was now even more absolute in contrast.

I thought you'd see a flash, he said to himself. But they did do it, right on time. The others do things.

He decided to lie down again but found himself so stiff and sore that the smallest movement made him wince. I'd better stay here till someone comes, he thought. One or another of his friends was bound to come soon to tell him what had happened. I'll ask them to lift me back on the bed with my damn leg.

II

AT SEVEN O'CLOCK that evening, a man whom the papers later identified only as "a young political criminal of unknown nationality" (but who was in reality the disowned son of one of the prominent families in the capital) had been shot dead by a detective of police as he pulled a bomb out of his pocket. He had been standing among the rather small crowd of on-lookers who had gathered to see the vice-president attend the gala opening of a patriotic play in the new theater. The young man had not known that his por-trait was carried by the men from the various "special departments" and that one of them had recognized him as soon as he had worked his way up to the front of the spectators. It would have been easy to arrest or search him right then, but as a minute later he pulled out the small metal cylinder—which was actually only a smoke bomb—the detective cocked his pistol and shot him through the head; the second shot was fired as a friend of the young man rushed up and started to wrestle with the detective. He was shot through the shoulder and taken to the police station. At his first interrogation, two of his ribs were fractured and he died in the night of a lung hemorrhage. The vice-president, whose carriage upon arrival was led to a side entrance, was not even told about the little drama until the first intermission.

"A.", the student with the broken leg (if he was generally called A., it was perhaps because his name started with an A, but certainly not from any attempt at secrecy) was told of all this later—except of course of the death of the arrested man which occurred at just about the time A. and his friends were discussing the events of that evening, and which would never be announced at all. There were some students in his room, men and girls, and a few older people, all members of the local committee of the Radical Party, a legal or illegal organization. No one, not even the chief of police, would really be able to say which. As an editorial in *The People* had put it,

The free interplay of political opinions is of the very essence to our modern, progressive nation, and gagging our opponents would smack of the Middle Ages . . . on the other hand, it is equally obvious that those who would obstruct our country's course can be as little tolerated as, say, a man who would want to obstruct the flow of traffic along our main avenue.

Because of A.'s broken leg, it was natural for them to come to his room, which was a popular meeting place anyway; they liked the security of the beehive building with all its staircases and sections. The unhappy ending of this demonstration by the others seemed to prove that violence, the threat of violence, even the threat of a minor disturbance, were self-defeating. That was Dr Wenster's point; "our aims must be achieved within the political machinery," he said. Although everyone present really agreed with him, nobody answered, for Wenster had the unfortunate habit of choosing words he couldn't pronounce properly, and his thinly lisped "machinery" was very irritating. Wenster was a political refugee from so many different countries that he sometimes awoke in the night in a panic, thinking that he had mistakenly gone back to one on the list; he was a good political journalist who had had a hand in several of the committee's publications. His various deportations had also made him somewhat of a liaison man with the Radical Parties in other capitals. These usually called themselves not Radicals but the Young Czechs, the Young Swiss, the Young et cetera; in Wenster's case the adjective "young" had to be understood symbolically.

"I think it proves the others should learn to throw their bombs more quickly," A. finally said, because his leg was hurting. No one reacted to that but Anne, his girl friend, who smiled at him and half whispered, "Poor darling."

III

A. HAD BROKEN his leg politically. The Radical Party had held a public meeting, in a town square (although far from the center of town, and bordered by an empty lot and a vocational school), for which the police had given permission or at least not specifically refused permission. But when the committee arrived —it had been an unexpectedly beautiful late summer evening—there was no one waiting but a group of men who looked alike and wore the same raincoats.

After the first words of the opening statement, always made by their most respectable member, a university professor of natural history, these men had started a disturbance; they first kicked over the table on the platform and then began breaking up the chairs which had been borrowed with so much trouble. A. had just been kicked by one of them and kicked back when someone shouted, "The police!", and for no quite logical reason the committee members had run in all directions. As A. dashed down the steep stone steps which led into the old town, he had seen one of the raincoat men follow him, and before he could brace himself he had been pushed and fallen some thirty feet. His friends had soon found him and half carried, half walked him to his room, for it was a commonly accepted belief that the police regularly checked with hospitals and doctors and picked up people who had had any kind of unorthodox accident.

It had been a strange experience for A., who had grown up as the only child in a family with some money—not nearly as much money as a generation earlier, but still some. (If his mother heard him cough in the night, he was kept home and the doctor sent for; in the first ten years of his life she must have taken his temperature at least twice a week for a grand total of a thousand times.)

And now here he was on his straw mattress in an attic room which had neither running water nor a toilet and for which the miserable rent hadn't even

been paid, his leg being set by a third-year medical
student while Anne and another girl ran down the
stairs for linen and hot water. They got a potful from
the café around the corner for a penny. His friends
were standing around, watching with fascination.

It had not been an altogether unpleasant experience.

Lying there and feeling the sweat run down from
his hair into his neck, he was without a trace of self-
pity—perhaps for the first time since he had been
turned out of the house by his father for refusing to
quit the Radical Party. There was an odd happiness in
the sudden awareness of owning nothing, not sharing
in any spoils of this world at all, being about as far
down as one can go, he felt. There was a literary
connotation to the scene: the straw, the oil lamp, the
pain, even. And these people wanted to help him
restore his body, maintain himself on earth—for no real
reason except that he was he.

IV

ANNE was A.'s girl friend only in the limited sense of
making love. When A. was still in high school learning
Latin, he had been desperately eager to make an
impression; like those of his classmates who could get
the money out of their parents, he spent hours getting
dressed the right way, sticking down his hair, chewing

mints, learning how to dance, and whatever else was
supposed to win a girl over. But although he was told
he was attractive—he was tall, a bit ungainly in those
years, with dark eyes—no woman ever seemed to pay
any attention to him.

But when he had been put out of his house, sold his
watch, pawned his dinner jacket and seen the other
clothes he had taken with him slowly disintegrate, he
became "successful"; perhaps because he was no
longer very eager himself: his new ideas prevented
that. But the success was only with girls of his own
group and seemed to conform to a pattern he saw
around him. Anne, for instance, who told him that she
loved him, was possibly only in love with the idea of
emancipation their relationship implied. She had not
been his first girl, but almost; and only with her did he
begin to learn properly about making love. She stayed
behind with him evenings and said good night to the
others with as little ado as a married woman. But once
in bed with him, or rather, on his straw mattress, she
seemed much more excited about it all than he, A.
thought. He very much enjoyed her and felt better for
it; but the title of a university lecture, "Sexual Hy-
giene," always came back to his mind. It was most
convenient, for he did not even have to get up to take
her home; she insisted on leaving alone. Nor did she
worry about the effort it took to make him answer "I
love you too" when she told him she loved him. He
was supposed to be an introvert young man. They

belonged to the same political committee, and thus they always met, with or without date; A. obviously was not expected to have money to take her out. In spring, A. thought, it would be more complicated; she'd expect him to take her on walks in the woods, rowing perhaps—what could he say then that would satisfy her, and what point was there in kissing her if they weren't going to make love? "What are you thinking about?" Anne asked and he truthfully answered, "You."

There was nothing affected about A.'s poverty. Although he still worked hard at the university, he had tried all sorts of outside jobs since his father had cut him off, but with a singular lack of results. There was too much unemployment and too much of a class barrier to give him a chance at any manual work. Foremen never looked twice at "student types." And if he ever came near a job as a crammer or translator, it was always spoiled the moment he gave his name: they knew all about him in the town. Only people from his own party were different, and they were as a rule almost as poor as he was. The drying up of the various sources which had kept him going during his exile from home was at hand: he had virtually nothing left to offer the municipal pawnshop, unpaid bills barred him from his former cafés and restaurants; after being thrown out by his father he had had one more suit made by their tailor (and then sold it) and could not hope to succeed in that again; his mother was in the country, staying with relatives, and had left three letters unanswered: they had probably been intercepted at his father's behest.

A. had moments—as when his leg was set—when he realized the aesthetics of this situation, but he usually hated his poverty. He had the tendency, unfortunate for a new member of the committee, to like if not the rich themselves, at least their activities and surroundings, and to dislike the poor; a woman in rags toting a baby, barefoot children, made him feel sadistic rather than compassionate.

His socialism, then, had the impatience or unfriendliness of a fashionable doctor forced to attend a tramp run over in the street.

V

HE LIKED to think of a division into a body world and a conscience world; in the first, the actuality of yourself was sharp and pleasurable; in the second, almost its cancellation, the only answer was that being alive did not matter. When he was younger, he had thought about a girl, women, almost abstractly; the idea behind the trivialities of wearing a good suit or saying something amusing at a party was vague, a romantic waiting for what was bound to happen. All that had vanished. He was convinced that the romanticness of those thoughts, tears shed by women in Turgenev stories, dreams arising out of music heard somewhere, were self-indulgences, egoistic and not *really* important. They were little luxuries of the body, as the narcissisms of philosophers in petty German towns were luxuries of the mind. They tempted but that was all.

His abstractions were now anatomic, Anne's body was important as an object to stroke, to stroke inside, stroking oneself in the same movements. He no longer thought of a woman but of a woman's thighs, of the mystery of his touching her. When he was still in his parents' house, he would go into their bedroom on Sundays when they had gone out and look at himself, sit on a chair as close as possible to the mirror; and the singularity of the thought that a woman would allow him to empty himself in her overwhelmed him. It was a pain almost, which he still felt and which was unchanged by the unimportance real love making seemed to have, listening to Anne's steps on the staircase as she went home in the night. All that, he thought, was not the animal side in man, for only with the civilization of clothing had this begun, the real intensity of sex, of just looking, even.

It was man's earthly, trivial side.

Not sin, simply trivial. Chemical dreams fostered by fluids or electric currents within oneself.

If that weren't so, if the body dream were not just created within itself, death would be a calamity. In his conscience world, death was no such thing.

His conscience world was what he called the panorama reaching to the ends of the world and down in time, which he could not stop himself from studying, the panorama of violence. In it men killed and tortured. Separated from each other by the unbridgeable gap of I-am-I, one man would use the awareness of his own body to create the maximum of pain in another body. He penetrated a weakness he only knew because it was his own, too; he played on an instrument he did not understand but only knew the reactions of. Men burned each other slowly, broke on wheels, killed with a hammer blow on the heart, tore off limbs. The Romans used to act out mutilation and death in their theaters with real men and women being mutilated and killed in reality, and when he was told that in school, he had thought that he would have gone too, that the whole town would go if they'd do it again that very night. To admit pleasure in killing had become rare; modern nations killed, tortured suspects, or worked men to death, for more serious purposes. But the senselessness of the separation between one man and another, the infinity between the man wielding the knife and the man flayed, only acquired sense and left him in peace if it did not matter.

If living did not matter, and if dying in a second, or in twenty-four hours, or six months, made no difference.

If living were to matter, the world had to be re-created.

VI

THERE WERE radiant days that fall, with a dark blue sky as seldom seen there, the rays of the setting sun just reaching around the corner of his building, almost parallel to his window ledge; when he stretched out his hand, it was enveloped in its light. But when A. could finally move about again in the street, it was November.

The first day he could walk without a crutch and without Anne's help, he went, not very sensibly, all the way to the river. The streets were muddy. It was early morning and the sidewalks were crowded with men going to work, women going to the market to shop. Light snow had fallen before dawn; now an intermittent drizzle covered everything with a film. Drops ran down his neck, his legs were sore, but he felt happy.

He leaned over the bridge parapet and looked at the swirling black water. A barge approached from upstream and he waited until the skipper had passed under him; the man frowned with concentration as he steered past the bridge column but when his eye caught A.'s, he shrugged, with a half-smile. I must look like a real bum, A. thought. There had been just that touch of compassion in the skipper's face for a tramp on a raw day. I'm working so hard because I'm an idiot too, that shrug said, we're all messing along the best we can. On se defend, as they say on the Seine.

He heard the voices of the pedestrians passing behind him, without distinguishing the words.

We'll do it, he thought. Contrary to all sense and expectation, we'll succeed, we'll set this town on edge, we will turn it upside down. Give me a fulcrum and I'll move the world; well, love will be our fulcrum, we'll use people's hearts, we'll dig them out from under the mud and dust and everything they're so afraid of. And suddenly it is going to be different. And why shouldn't it? The book is wrong of course, it isn't even in the interest of a few men, the way things are now—the rich, the generals, the politicians, they aren't really happy. My father isn't. They're just huddling in their shelter. And thus they're better off than the poor who don't have a shelter. But the news, my news, is that there is no need for shelter. There is no storm. We're all too damn grim.

It will be a hard job to tell that to them. He turned around. Just look at them, look at their hurrying along to their offices, where their coats will steam and smell all day, and so will they.

Wouldn't it be better just to get out of here?

He did not know his answer to that. If an eccentric British millionaire had right then tapped him on the shoulder to engage him as his traveling secretary, because he liked A.'s face, he might have accepted.

He fished a letter out from under his wet overcoat.

It was addressed to Anne. He had written it in the night; it had been hard work. In it he told her that he liked her very much but that it had not been true when he had said, "I love you"; he simply liked sleeping with her. He tore it up and dropped the pieces over the wall; the wind caught them before they reached the water and blew them under the bridge. I should have thrown them over the other parapet across the street, he thought, with the wind behind me. One of the reasons he had torn up the letter probably was to see it float down the river. There would have been something satisfactory in that picture.

I should start right now, climb up here and deliver my first speech. They'd think I was going to commit suicide and arrest me. Or more likely, one of them would push me in.

Where do you start? How can you talk about love unless you're Jesus? Perhaps better stick to Marx after all. But he's as grim as everyone here, he must have worn just that dreary sort of schoolteacher's coat that man there has on. We need a well-dressed revolutionist with a sense of humor. Like the Count of Saint-Simon, is that who it was? Whatever became of him? I must ask Anne. But why would things precisely now, precisely in that speck in eternity which is my time, change? You must admit, it's a damned unlikely thing to expect, the odds are a million to one. But electric light was invented in my time. Why not general happi-

ness? Now *there* is a program for the winter campaign.
Gentlemen, we have invented human happiness. We
propose the conversion from misery to happiness,
much as from gaslight to electricity. Hurrah. Lock up
that madman. Vagueness is the curse of revolutions.
But one song does more than ten manifestoes.

It was such a beautiful town. It had a somber, an
archaic, feudal, beauty, but no other kind existed yet;
perhaps no other kind was possible; beauty was based
on exclusivity. The towers everywhere, of churches
and castles, loomed through the rain. Severe, pure
lines, an enviable hardness; no connection between
them and the clerks with the wet feet. No connection
between them and anything. We're all a bunch of
clods. The politicians, the senators, were terribly
wrong if they thought these towers were they. Nothing and no one of the present day would ever fit
against that background again but a civil war, a peas-
ant rebellion marching into town with torches and
rapine. Such a spectacle the towers would recognize
and look down upon benevolently.

VII

THE TIME for elections to the Assembly came up and
the papers wrote that although these elections were
not based on proportional representation and were

somewhat less than direct, they nevertheless assured
the people that they were heard. The entire country
could not be seated in the Assembly, ha ha. Those
who were seated would not speak for themselves.
Their voices would have the strength of thousands.

The others, as A.'s committee always referred to
them, had no policy but to boycott the entire proceedings. They had had a broadside printed in which they
said that political democracy, remote as it was, was
worn out anyway; in which they talked about eco-
nomic sovereignty of the people and stated their pref-
erence for a downright tyranny over the hypocritical
farces of the day. "Voters," it ended, "you are like dogs
wagging their tails as their master offers them a
choice of nice new collars."

"I like that about the collars," Anne said.

But none of them ever saw such a broadside handed
out in the street; theirs had been brought by Wenster
who was pledged not to say where he got it. The
newsboy at the corner of the quay gave one out with
every newspaper sold one morning, but that did not
last very long. He swore he didn't know where they
were from and had thought they were advertisements
such as the paper sometimes included. He was fired all
the same, and a policeman was dispatched for house
search. It turned out the boy had no house, and the
officer spent the allotted hour drinking in a café, and
came back looking flushed and pleased with himself.
He sat down and wrote his report which said, "There
was nothing there."

A.'s committee decided to be less sullen than the others. They couldn't very well campaign for any of the Deputies, but they could use the occasion to speak about general suffrage, every man a vote, against the military mind, that kind of thing: let themselves be heard. And why not. They could even carefully endorse one or two candidates who were least far removed from their point of view, explaining as they did so why they were endorsing such and such a person, use him to smuggle in some ideas of their own.

And money wasn't as much of a problem as they expected; five hundred francs arrived from abroad; their professor put up fifty, Wenster thirty, and many students, including Anne, two or three. That was it; but there was a printer who would work free evenings and give paper, they would have a travel fund, print posters for their meetings, and put out a pamphlet. The police commissioner received three of them and explained how the town welcomed political awareness for all its citizens during the coming weeks. "After all, everyone of us loves his country," he said gloomily. He passed cigarets around and even regretted that two students had been beaten up a few days earlier outside a factory. They had been on private property and thus he could hardly do anything about it. "Then we may assume . . ." the professor began, but he was stopped by a kick under the table; it was better to assume in silence.

There were handshakes.

"He's not so bad, really," one of them said outside.

"He follows orders. He's as bad as his orders. He's nothing."

"I think he has a sense of humor," the university professor said hopefully. "When he made that remark about our students being on private property, he winked at me."

"He did?"

"I think so."

VIII

A. HAD ASKED for a chance to be a speaker. He was frightened but he had promised it to himself; that was his "bridge decision." The committee was not wildly enthusiastic about the offer, but since he was so eager —and had, after all, broken his leg at their last meeting—they gave him a little industrial town, fifty miles from the capital, for a try. They had no one there, but a local café owner had made his bowling alley available and would hang a poster; a boy could pass out leaflets at the factory and in the market.

It was only three in the afternoon when A. got off the train at his destination. The meeting was scheduled for six, after the day shift of the factory. There were no other passengers, not even a ticket collector at the exit gate. Some road workers were throwing boulders from a flatcar. They grunted and panted. It was a fantastic presumption to address such men. A. was shaking—from the bitter cold in the wooden train compartment, he said to himself. It had been a deadening trip with its innumerable stops where no one got on or off.

He came out on the station square.

In its center stood a stone equestrian, pointing his sword at the public toilets. An icy wind blew sand across the open space; four empty and silent little streets radiated into the town. To the west, where the sun had already set, the sky was black and purple with the factory smoke. A. found someone to give him directions and set out for the café, still walking halt-ingly, while mumbling, "Gentlemen, you are here . . ." "Friends, we in the capital . . ." "Ladies and Gentlemen, I thank you for your presence. Soon . . ."

When he opened the café door, a little bell rang as in a candy store. The owner was sitting near the stove, his feet up, reading a book.

He looked over it at A.

"I'm from the Radical Party," A. said.

"Are all of you so young?"

A. shrugged. The café owner sat upright and had another look at him. "You dressed the part, didn't you?" he asked, but in a very gentle voice. "Wanted to look like one of them."

"It's my best suit," A. answered and sat down. He had been given some expense money. "Do you think you could give me a sandwich, and a beer?"

"Better make it a little gin," the owner said. "Beer is a fidgety drink for men who have to do public speaking."

"How do I address them?" A. asked after a while.

The café owner looked at him with some surprise.

"I mean, 'Ladies and Gentlemen,' or 'Gentlemen,' or 'Friends'?"

The café owner closed his book. " 'Ladies and Gentlemen' won't be needed," he said. "There'll be no ladies present. If you had set your hopes on that, you'll be disappointed. 'Friends' doesn't sound so good either. Why 'Friends'? They're not your friends. Why would they be?"

A. did not answer that.

"The other lot, the real ones, say 'Brothers,' " the café owner went on. "But that wouldn't sound right from you. You're too—eh—towny. Too studenty. Though I grant you those elbows are almost worn through. I'd just start if I were you. Don't address them with anything."

"Why do you call the others 'the real ones'?" A. asked.

"Well, they are, you know. The Reds, I mean, the real socialists. They say, occupy the factory. It's yours. They're right of course. What else can you do? The rest is just talk."

"Why do you give us your hall then?"

"Oh, I don't know. To annoy the factory manager. He's a real bastard. I surely couldn't have the revolutionaries in here. My place would be closed like a shot. Or the least that would happen, my windows smashed."

A. emptied his gin and got up to study the poster which had been hung against the glass of the door. "A speaker from the committee in the capital," it said. The place and the day had been filled in by hand. He sat down at a table near the door, took a sheet of paper from his pocket and started to make notes. The café owner studied him.

"You know," he then said, "don't have your hopes too high. There won't be that many coming."

"How many?" A. asked, keeping his voice business-like.

"Oh, I don't know. Ten or fifteen, maybe."

"Ten or fifteen!" A. cried. He had seen himself, half exalted and half horrified by the vision, addressing a room packed with hundreds of men.

The owner laughed. "Thirty, maybe, drop in here after the shift. A few will be curious enough to get up to hear you. I'll tell you what. Open that door, that's the place, behind there. I'll poke up the stove. If it's cold in there, they won't stay long."

"Can't we stay in here?"

"That's against the law."

"Won't anyone from the town come?"

"Yes, perhaps," the owner said unconvincingly. "It's going to be a queer lot anyway. The foremen and such don't come here. They go across the street." He nodded toward the door. "The real miseries won't come either. They can't afford a drink—only on pay-day. You'll get sort of a middling lot. They read, though. They know what's up. Why don't you have another gin, I'll join you. And cheer up, boy. Just tell them what you've come all that way for. Tell them what you think they must hear."

"Gentlemen," A. said, and took a deep breath. Thank God, no one seemed to have been bothered by that. "You're here not to listen to some student who knows less about life than you. You're here to listen to the national committee of the Radical Party. I speak for them. If we had the money, the entire committee, the whole committee—"

It is dark, ashen dark, with a lingering smell of the lamp and the evening meal; the air is stone cold; the bed, worse, is moist and cold. It's the first factory whistle. He crawls out from under the cover, puts on his trousers and struggles his swollen stockinged feet, chilblains, into his boots. A figure in the bed, his wife, is still asleep, she groans—snores? coughs with tuber-culosis? The child, children, whimper. He picks up a chunk of bread and the tin bottle of water, and comes out into the street. The sky is lightening. He rinses his mouth from the bottle. He walks toward the renewed screaming of the factory.

"This is not a war, gentlemen." (I must cut out that gentlemen stuff). "It is a siege. We are besieging the bastions of power. They look unassailable. Nothing stirs. One of us jumps up and runs toward the wall. Not a chance. He's shot down. But—"

When the machines start up, it is certain that no one will be able to stand that piercing, bullying, vibration for five minutes, let alone twelve hours; sweat already runs in his eyes. He peers through the steam and tries to decipher the dial on the clock in the foreman's office. It is only seven.

"Savonarola, the Italian reformer—when the rulers of Florence couldn't even pretend any more that they were playing along with him, they arrested him; for heresy, I think. That is the medieval word for sedition. And as they started to burn him, a gust of wind blew the flames away. 'A miracle!' the people in the square shouted. They were all ready to believe in him once more—a bit disappointed too, they were, I don't doubt; to be cheated out of a nice execution. But then the wind dropped, and he burned. There are no such miracles—"

As he walks back toward the factory after the midday meeting, there is a ring of soldiers around the workshop. Someone must have given the alarm. No strikes are allowed, a national emergency, strikers drafted into the army.

The workmen hesitate. There are shouts, "Don't stop!"

He walks toward the pointed rifles; a rifle seen in foreshortening is a fearful tool. A red face behind it is grinning. Or perhaps it is just a leer, a grimace of doubt.

Perhaps the face is pale. Perhaps it's his own face.

"That wasn't half bad," the café owner said. "Honestly not, not half bad. They liked that bit about Savonarola."

IX

THE WEEK that followed saw a change of mood in the capital. It would have been hard to define what exactly had changed; it was a cumulative impression of a dozen trivialities. The political evenings organized by the candidates to address the voters unrolled in painfully hollow halls; even in the hearty editorials of *The People* a certain worry about the lack of response could be found between the lines. There had always been more than enough favor holders and favor seekers to fill those halls twice over; why didn't they make their appearance? Then the day the president was to visit the new iron foundry, more than half the workers reported sick and didn't show up, and the visit had to be canceled to avoid embarrassment. The Radical university professor, used to lecturing for half a dozen graduates, one morning found his auditorium packed with young people he had never seen and had to move his audience to a larger room; after he had spoken his usual fifty minutes, on ecology, he received, startled, an ovation. The two meetings for which the Radical Party had received a permit drew so many people that the familiar faces of the habitués were lost among them.

On Main Avenue, in morning hours accustomed only to ladies in carriages, elderly gentlemen strollers, and governesses with children, now were seen groups of students who should have been in class, and men in working clothes, not doing anything obvious, but present, as if taking stock.

A feeling of unrest pervaded the heart of the city, unaffected by the cold rain and wind which swept over it day after day. The rich stayed home evenings. Ladies took off their jewelry before going out to tea. Shopkeepers were seen boarding up their windows as soon as the early dusk fell. But nothing happened, not a stone was thrown.

At the committee, a sense of euphoria descended. For no solid reason, everyone had decided that this was the moment. They all did and said more or less the same things as earlier in the year, but now it was not a going through motions, it was life itself. Of a sudden, the vaguest goals seemed in reach. There were meetings all the time, in one place or another, and without fail someone would come running in with a wild rumor, the president had resigned, there was a general strike in the north, the new assembly would demand a revision in the constitution. None of it turned out to be true the following morning; all of it seemed possible to each of them for one evening and one night.

The day before the election there was to be a government rally in Central Square. They were going to hold a counter-rally at the same hour, not of course presenting it as such, but simply as a public meeting, "A summing up of the lessons to be drawn from the campaign." They had rented a hall from a gymnastics club, far on the outskirts of town, almost in the countryside; but there was a terminal of the omnibus service opposite it.

On the morning of that last day the papers reported, in identical terms, "A frontier incident in the town of Z—." The name was not spelled out. A serious situation might develop, it was said, and political activities tending to disunite rather than unite the country were immediately proscribed.

The committee decided not to cancel their evening in the hall.

They had already paid their rent to the gymnasts. One of the members pointed out that no frontier post of the country had a name starting with Z.

X

THEY TOOK TURNS going downtown to check; there was nothing to report. But it was quieter than the day before and the area around the main government buildings lay almost deserted. At six o'clock, two hours before the meeting was to start, a breathless student showed up and announced, "They've closed the hall."

It was rush hour, and it took them fifty minutes to get there. There were no lights on in the building, and no one was in sight until the committee members came up across the dark little park in front of it, some of them almost running. Then half a dozen policemen appeared from various corners. "This building cannot be used," a police sergeant told them.

"Why not?" the professor asked, automatically stepping into his liaison role with the worldly powers.

"I don't know," the sergeant said. "Fire regulations perhaps. You can't hang around here, though."

"What is going on, officer?" a man asked, appearing out of the dark.

The sergeant sized him up from his hat to his neat black gaiters. "Nothing for you to concern yourself with, sir," he then said. "Some student business."

"But I am concerned," the man answered. "I've come for the meeting."

The professor groaned. The fact that such a dapper gentleman would have been the first member of the public to enter the hall made its closing that much more painful to him.

"The meeting?" the sergeant repeated. "But the meeting is in Central Square."

Those of the committee who heard this began to laugh, but then one of them said, "So it is. Let's go there."

Central Square, ringed by banks and insurance companies, was never a particularly animated part of the town at night. Now it was bathed in light; the speakers' platform had electric lamps, and all over the square brightly blue-white carbide lamps had been hung. When the platform was not producing sound, the lamps' hissing in chorus could be heard, for the wind had died down that evening and the audience was very still. The square was filled with benches which were neither full nor empty; only in front of the rostrum every place was taken. Ladies, dressed in the national colors, were standing in the aisles, ready to usher any late arrivals; policemen and national guardsmen formed a black outer circle. Beyond them the wide avenues of the financial district lay quiet but for the steps of a few patrolling policemen. Normally, their new electric streetlights made them seem well lit; now in contrast to the glare of the square, they had acquired a softer shadowiness. From above, the pattern must have looked like a white spider with grey legs.

Along one of these streets, the committee members came to the square. They were marching fast and A., whose leg hurt, was trailing behind; he had lost Anne, who was walking with some old lady from a provincial town. The silent policemen along the avenue hardly looked at them. They could hear the booming voice of a speaker and see the white rings of the lamps through the bare branches of the trees; then they were at the outer circle. The police and the guards immediately stepped aside, and the patriotic ladies pounced on them with delight. They were all put on one bench, quite close to the rostrum. The speaker finished, there was scattered applause, and three musicians in leather shorts appeared and began playing accordions.

A. sat at the end of the bench, and as he looked sideways at his fellow members, he saw there was a huddle of whispers in the middle.

"This great city—"

The musicians had vanished and the mayor of the capital himself had begun speaking without A.'s realizing it; he had been too busy installing his leg under the bench before him. His neighbor nudged him; as he looked, he saw that Wenster had climbed up on the bench and that several others were following his example. The bench wobbled; some of the committee men were balancing themselves with difficulty. Up front, heads were turned at the strange spectacle of these dark figures with arms outstretched against the light. The mayor saw it too, and hesitated; he clearly did not know what he was watching. "I can't get up on this bench," A. said somewhat plaintively to the man next to him, "not with my leg." But his neighbor paid no attention to him. Wenster had found his balance and he was now waving his hat at the mayor. The mayor stopped speaking.

"Mr Mayor!" Wenster shouted in his terrible accent which sounded quite heart-warming now, A. thought, "Mr. Mayor, a question! Why isn't the Deputy for the Northeast here tonight? Is it true, then, that he was bribed at the instigation of—"

That was as far as Wenster got, for one of the guards had now reached him from behind and knocked him off the bench with one elbow. In that same moment, policemen were behind all of them, pulling them back over the bench and out of the square. There was complete silence; the rest of the audience stared blankly at them. You'd have expected we'd scream and protest, A. thought. Then the accordion music struck up again. The mayor had stepped back, and A. could see the men in the leather shorts cheerfully pulling and pushing at their instruments as he was dragged backward through the outer circle which closed behind him. Under the fierce blue lamps and the weakly metallic music, the scene had looked like anything but a demonstration—more like some modern industrial ballet.

XI

THE SHOCK for A. came not when he was arrested but when he was released.

He had not been concerned when they were marched off in little groups to a police station he had never noticed before, in the wing of a municipal building. That, to the contrary, had the relief of a battle finally joined. At the station, they were separated from one another; as he was questioned, he thought of all the others going through this at that same time. He was pleased with himself, pleased to be *present;* we're here for everyone, we're a vanguard in our haphazard sort of way. This is much better than another meeting at that damn gymnasium. He felt sure of himself and felt he was answering the questioning with fine irony.

Then he was taken to a little room with only a chair in it and the door was locked behind him. There was no way to turn off the light, but in the end he fell asleep sitting on the floor, with his head against the wall.

He woke up when the door was unlocked, and scrambled onto his feet with difficulty. He felt awful. A policeman stood there and made a gesture with his head to follow him. "I want to wash my face and go to the toilet," A. said. The policeman muttered something and led A. through a long corridor. Dirty windows let in the morning light. The man opened a door. Beyond it was an alley full of garbage cans.

A. stared at him.

"You can go home," the policeman said impatiently, and as A. stepped across the threshold, the door was closed and locked behind him.

A. had braced himself for another interrogation, and he had prepared a good speech, he thought. He had been prepared to be beaten too. The one thing he had not expected was to find himself in the street again.

It was a miserable morning, and as he hastened through the alley and turned the corner, a hard, wet wind hit him and blew through his clothes. Then he was on one of the main shopping streets of the town.

It was crowded with women and children; Christmas decorations everywhere swayed and rattled in the wind. "Watch it," a delivery man shouted at him. He stepped aside and found himself in the doorway of a tearoom. He opened the door; a liveried doorman who had been standing inside warming himself hastily barred his way. "Where you going?" he said. "I—" A. began. He then realized that he had no money and that his pants were sagging. The night before they had taken away his belt and shoelaces. For a moment he thought he'd snidely inform the man that he used to have tea with his mother in that place every week, as a child. Instead he turned around and walked out again; in the street, he looked in the mirror in the tearoom window. It was worse than he had imagined; his face was stubbly and dirty from the floor he had slept on; his eyes were swollen. But his main problem right then, it seemed to him, was to get to a toilet. It would be an hour back to his room on foot. He wondered if all of them were set free. Anne surely, if they had let him go. What about Wenster? But he couldn't wait here.

He tried to remember who on the committee lived nearby, and couldn't think of anyone. He was dizzy; he had not eaten since the morning of the day before. For a moment he was tempted to put out his hand and try and beg some money.

He leaned against the restaurant window and watched the passers-by.

How they hurried, how preoccupied they all were! And how happy they seemed! They were all talking and thinking of Christmas, that was to say, of *things,* of buying and having and giving things, of money, of big dinners, of trips, of clothes.

No one even glanced at him.

But what fools we are, he said to himself. What fools we were with our election. What an idiot I was yesterday with my vanguard, what a stupid fool. They don't give a shit. And it wouldn't be on page ten of the paper if they had knocked my head in at the rally. If you want to clown, they think, go ahead, clown. We know it's election day today and we know why we don't care.

He had been self-possessed standing under a bare lightbulb across the desk of a policeman with the face of a bully. Now, in this crowded shopping street, he was shaken.

He felt more alone than he ever remembered having been.

He took a step back and was struck by the tearoom door opened by someone coming out.

"I beg your—" a crisp lady's voice began, but as she saw that she had hit some kind of tramp, her voice dropped and the "pardon" was almost inaudible. "Come, Helen," she said over her shoulder to a young girl who had followed her out, and hastily turned right.

The girl made a little sidestep to avoid touching A. He looked at her. Her face had an expression, not of aversion or contempt, simply of a moment's irritation at being confronted with one of the less pleasing aspects of life. Their eyes met; she frowned.

Behind him, the doorman came outside and said, "Come on now, fellow, you're bothering our customers."

He stared after her without hearing.

XII

A GIRL'S FACE.

He hated her totally: he hated the complacency, the untouchableness; she was the shoppers, the blandly staring neighbors as Wenster was knocked off his bench; she was the enemy. She was the temptation, the way of least resistance, the easy life. How she made sure she wasn't going to brush against me! he thought. She has no idea I could be sitting in that damned tearoom too if I had wanted that, that I could still make it to the Christmas Ball if I went to see my father now—This is Helen. Delighted. Would you care to dance?

It's easy for Wenster, he said to himself, Wenster had nothing to lose.

But that is the voice of the devil, telling me that.

How can we get Wenster out of jail?

She had such a beautifully pure face. How unjust it was; it was given to her by nature, perchance, but she looked out from it as if it couldn't have been otherwise, as if she had a right to it, a right to be above all the troubles flesh is heir to. There was nothing earthy about her.

With Anne you knew if she was cold or hungry or had got up in too much of a hurry to wash properly.

Anne's face would have puckered, coming out into a cold wind like that. It was easy to feel sorry for her.

I wish I could seduce that girl, but literally. That would avenge Anne, and me, and us all.

Thus he came back to his building.

He had to pull himself together to climb all the stairs. Anne and several others were in his room, talking. Someone had brought food and beer, which made a marvelous sight on the table.

XIII

"YOU'RE THE LAST ONE," A. was told as he flopped down on his mattress, "we're all out but Wenster."

"They'll deport him," A. said.

He closed his eyes and he was standing again in front of that tearoom. But then with a great effort he shook himself to stay awake.

They were talking about Wenster.

"They'll let you pick your own border at times."

"At times."

"I thought Wenster wanted to work within the political machinery."

Someone laughed uneasily.

"But of course he was within the machinery. If you can't ask questions at a political rally—"

"What about the election, anyway?"

"Oh, the election—"

A silence.

The professor said, "I had been thinking along these lines. Indeed, Wenster was only asking a question, and no one can even say exactly how he was going to end it."

"And?"

"I was thinking of Gansard."

There was a more or less cultural weekly, called something like *The New Reader*, or *The Reader's Friend*, which was owned and edited by Gansard, a disreputable, rather alcoholic, political columnist. But surprisingly, he did not always toe one of the various acceptable lines. Several explanations for this liberty circulated; the most romantic one had it that he was the natural son of the retired former president of the country, General-of-the-Army W. A more probable explanation held that this was controlled minor opposition, indirectly paid for by the government through a weekly advertisement from the Bureau of Iron Manufactures. Yet Gansard was supposed to have some influence.

"We have two hundred francs left."

The professor nodded gravely.

"Are you going to see him, Professor?"

"No, not him; it should be someone not known."

"Who looks innocent and respectable."

One by one, they came to look at A.

He stared back at them and then, realizing what

they thought, sat upright on his mattress. "Oh no," he said, "not me. I've had it for today."

"Oh come on, A., why not? Wouldn't you do that for Wenster?"

"I—I've something else to do today," A. answered. He had planned to lie on his mattress when they had all gone, and think of this girl Helen. He had looked forward to that. Idiotic, and he could not help reddening.

They saw it. "He has nothing to do," one man said determinedly, "and he does look innocent."

"But certainly not respectable," A. protested. "Look at me."

"We'll fix you up."

XIV

IT BECAME A GAME "to fix up A." Everyone ran off to fetch odds and ends of tailoring elegance. The somber mood which had weighed on the room was suddenly gone; these students, usually so serious and old, now thought it was hilarious to bedeck A. as respectably as possible for his visit to bribe the magazine editor. He had to shave under general scrutiny, and sit up with a towel around his neck while Anne gave him a haircut. He had a good pair of shoes himself, but all his other possessions were rejected; he had to borrow one man's

suit, a beautiful white shirt with a ruffled front from
another, a red silk tie, and the coat of the professor,
who was not amused but did not protest. And since
wet snow had started falling, they even went to get an
umbrella for him; he had to arrive dry for his mission.

A. was immediately shown into Gansard's office,
where the editor was slouched in an easy chair and
not doing anything. A. introduced himself and waited
for Gansard to ask what he had come for; but Gansard
was content to chew on his wet cigar. A., however,
had carefully rehearsed how he was going to present
the case as forcefully as possible, and how to mention
money without offending the editor. They had made
quite a point of that in his room before they let him
go.

"I've come to see you about the case of Dr
Wenster," A. finally said. "He was arrested last night
when he—"

"Yes, I know about it," Gansard interrupted.

"We have been asking ourselves if the *Reader's* . . .
if your paper would be interested in discussing the
case," A. went on after another silence. "We could
give you a lot of background material on it—we
realize political articles are difficult—but after all, the
government did talk about 'a new political awareness.'
I've seen those precise words printed somewhere. We
were invited to a new— We hold then, that Wenster
was simply doing his invited duty when he tried to
foster a debate and . . ." A. had had trouble continu-

ing and now he let his voice trail off, for Gansard was not listening.

"Does your committee have funds for publicity?" the editor suddenly asked.

"Yes, indeed," A. hastily said, "I've two hundred francs with me, earmarked for that."

"Well, leave them on the table there," Gansard said, "and I'll see—we'll write something."

When A. came outside, the sleet had become snow and the street and the trees were already white. When he put the money down on the side table, he had taken one of Gansard's cigars—stolen it, rather, for the editor had certainly no thought of offering them. It had been a little gesture of inimicality because Gansard hadn't even bothered to go through the pretensions of probity, but perhaps, he thought, that means he's no hypocrite.

He pulled the coat collar up against his neck and put the cigar in his mouth. He was aware how dapper he looked, compared to the morning; he didn't really long to look that way at all any more, he discovered, but it was amusing, it was sort of a masquerade.

The air was clear and cold. He took a deep breath; he felt wide awake and pleased with himself. He wasn't going back yet to his room. If he only had some money!, he'd better start planning something if he wanted to eat the next day; he couldn't mooch on Anne. Who would lend him ten francs? He would think about it at home.

He went back inside to get a light for his cigar, then changed his mind, carefully wiped the mouthpiece dry and put it in his pocket. Because he was so aware of his neat appearance, he set out for the tearoom of that morning.

In the light snow, the shopping street now seemed quite charming. The tinsel decorations were happily covered with white; the snowflakes made the shoppers appear more innocent and less intense. It was even more crowded than when he had first seen it that day, and he looked the passing ladies in the face, smiling at himself. One or two of them smile back, he thought, how about that.

At the tearoom, the doorman was standing outside, dressed splendidly now in red with a fur collar and hat.

"I wonder if you can help me," A. said, pulling out the Gansard cigar and handing it to the doorman. He didn't do it too badly; as it came out, it looked like one of many. The doorman would rather have had a tip, but he accepted the cigar. He did not recognize A. from their first meeting of the day; he looked at people's clothes only.

"A young lady, an acquaintance of mine, had tea here this morning with her mother," A. told him. "I was to join them but I couldn't make it."

The doorman began to look dubious. "Excuse me," he said and went to open a door for an arriving customer.

"I have to send them a note of apology, you see," A. went on when the doorman was at his post again, "because I'm going back to the country tonight. We live in the country." Leaving tonight, no nonsense planned; live in the country, respectable. "But the problem is, I don't think I have her last name right. There were so many people in our house Sunday. . . . It's Helen, Helen Fournier, something like that."

The doorman had almost lost his suspicious look but he did not know any Helen Fournier.

"Wait," A. said, "Fournier was her cousin perhaps, or was it. Look, her mother is a biggish woman, often in black, with light furs and so. The girl wears a tweed sports coat, English. Very handsome girl, grey-blue eyes."

"You don't mean Mrs Peret, sir?" the doorman asked, cheering up. "Her daughter's name is Helen, I think. And they were here this morning, but they didn't seem to be waiting for anyone."

"Mrs Peret," A. repeated slowly. "Does she live on Ring Avenue?"

"Oh no, they live on South Hill. But why don't you ask the cashier?"

"Well, no, I'll let it go," A. said. "Thank you very much, anyway."

He set out for South Hill, but as he had crossed the bridge and started up the very long and steep boulevard which circled the park, it was getting dark, and his shoes began to leak. I've done enough for one time, he decided, I'd better go home and report on Gansard.

To know her name meant having some kind of power over her.

XV

WHEN he came out of the last seminar before the Christmas recess, a note was given to A. by the porter. It was from his mother who was in town and who with excessive complexity had arranged a meeting in an out-of-the-way restaurant. She arrived trembling, for she was mortally afraid of her husband. After a while she calmed down and they had a much better time together than when A. was still living at home; she treated him like a man. She still made him eat more than he wanted to, but he had indeed become very thin. Afterward she insisted on putting him on an omnibus and waving him off; and as A. stood on the back platform and the conductor rang the bell, he felt a wave of tenderness toward her go through him. "I do love you, you know," he said to her. She smiled at him. Once he was home and took off his coat, he found that she had put a hundred-franc note in his pocket. He turned around and went out into the street again.

Half an hour later he stood facing the house where Helen Peret lived. It was the middle of the afternoon.

The streets were so quiet there that the rattle of the downtown traffic from below the park could be heard, rising along the hillside like invisible smoke.

The house was not as depressingly rich in appearance as he had expected; for that neighborhood, it was modest. Although the hundred-franc note had made him go there, it was unchanged in his pocket. He had not really wanted to use it for anything connected with that visit, and he now looked only slightly less disheveled than the morning she had seen him. He had no idea what he was going to do, but he felt it was somehow of the essence for him to make a dent in her complacency.

It is a *political* necessity for me, he thought, otherwise I'll hate the committee for it. That odd juxtaposition made sense to him.

He crossed the street and pulled the doorbell. He could hear it echo through the house, then steps, then a maid opening the door.

"I'm the tutor in Latin for Miss Helen," he said.

"Eh—this way," the maid said and opened the door.

He stood in a little drawing room, furnished very neatly with chairs in red silk and a small table of inlaid woods. There was a fire burning. He walked over to the window and looked out with a frown at the silent street. He could not hear a sound in the house, only the beating of his heart. He half turned around; to see her come in, he thought, and have my back to the light. But no one came.

After a while—it seemed an hour to him—his nervousness and anticipation had both gone. He had given up his strategic position and was sitting huddled near the fire. He just didn't want to wait in that room any longer; he almost imagined that he was indeed the tutor who was thus kept waiting.

The front door opened and closed, and there were voices; he jumped up as the girl came in.

His first feeling, painfully strong, was one of disappointment, at her appearance. I'm crazy, he thought, I was in a fever that morning. She is not so divine, she is just a girl like any other.

She had come in hastily, probably indignantly, but his sober stare disconcerted her somewhat. "There must be a mistake," she said, much more politely than she might have intended to, "I have no Latin tutor."

"Well, indeed," A. answered, "then why did they keep me waiting in here for an hour?"

"But who sent you?" she asked.

"No one *sent* me," A. said, offended.

She looked at him, then turned around, to summon the maid's help, he thought.

"The university bureau gave me this address," A. added more gently. "I'm a student and I give private lessons."

The girl was no longer worried now. "I'm very sorry," she said. "They made a mistake. I graduated from high school two years ago. And I've forgotten all my Latin, thank heaven." She laughed.

"Well, I'm sorry too, then. And I apologize for disturbing you." He walked past her, bowed, and let himself out.

Back on the street, he cursed himself. He should have—what? Stayed for tea? I could at least have laughed when she laughed. She had indeed been beautiful at that moment.

XVI

THE FOLLOWING AFTERNOON, but an hour later, he went again to the house. He walked past it twice before he rang the bell.

"The tutor," he said to the maid and walked into the little room.

"But, sir," the maid began, then turned around and hastily went up the stairs.

As he saw the girl come down, he lost his nerve, walked toward the front door and waited for her there, holding the door already open.

She stopped in the corridor. "It's a joke or something, is it?" she asked half-heartedly.

He looked at her, turning pale. "I lied yesterday," he said softly. "Not about being a student. I study under Professor Saitzew."

She opened her mouth and closed it again.

"I came here because I followed you," A. went on

with some effort. "I saw you once before, in a tearoom. I can't forget your face. I'm in love with you."

The girl blushed scarlet, then turned around and ran up the staircase.

He smiled idiotically at the maid who stood staring at him and who did not react. He shrugged and then left the house.

It doesn't matter a damn, he decided, no one will ever know. I've done what I wanted to do. She brushed against me after all.

XVII

THE ELECTION RESULTS were published, and *The People* made a labored attempt to show that they mattered and that something would be different.

Nothing was. The mood of freeness in the town, that contagious excitement, had totally vanished, and seemed like a dream now, set elsewhere.

Nothing further was ever written about any frontier incident, but many soldiers appeared in the capital (Christmas leave, the papers called it)—recruits from other regions, sons of farmers who marched the streets in groups. These new soldiers looked awkward and almost pathetic in their big boots and badly cut uniforms, staring about them at the life of the city; but there was a sprinkling of old noncoms of an entirely different race, men who walked, looked at the passers-by, and even sat in café chairs with an air of occupiers rather than defenders.

All sorts of army benefits were promoted.

The public was asked to invite a soldier for dinner, and a poster appeared showing an infantry man staring into the distance over his rifle sight while civilians were finding security in little red-windowed houses behind his large back.

Gansard's editorial appeared, *On the need for debate, in a conservative nation.* It had some mixed metaphors about draining off poisons before they could blossom into red flowers, but it said in so many words that Dr Wenster's detention was unjust. There was a stir in the cafés, but no official reaction followed.

Then, just before Christmas, a note from Wenster was smuggled out to the committee in which he told them he was to be put across the northern border the following morning. The northern frontier post nearest the capital was on a road parallel to the new railway bridge. It was the traditional spot where political refugees and deportees were shuttled back and forth between the two countries, and it was the worst place to have been chosen for Wenster, who once was deported there from north to south. If caught north of the border, he might be shot. A., who had been acting annoyed with himself, without Anne or anyone knowing why, announced unexpectedly that he was willing

to try to bring Wenster back—if they'd find the money
for train fares and if a note with instructions could be
smuggled back into prison. He would know how to
pick up Wenster across the frontier; he was familiar
with that part of the country, he used to camp there as
a boy long ago, before that border was virtually
closed.

Two hours later he was on the train, carrying food
and a botany kit from one of the other students, which
made a nice unspoken explanation of his purpose,
though a bit dubious in midwinter.

The early twilight was closing in when he got off at
the next to last stop before the frontier, a junction
with a few houses across from it. Looking neither left
nor right, he set out on foot along the country road
that ran beside the tracks and then veered west.
Petty officials like the junction man pacing up and
down the platform to keep warm and a rural guard
who sat in a shed near a stove, chewing tobacco, were
less inclined to ask questions of a person who showed
no hesitation in his movements.

Soon he had left all signs of human life behind him.

There was a sudden rift in the black clouds piling
up on each other over the western horizon, and
through it the setting sun appeared; a strange, oval
sun, purple and dead, and its last rays threw long
shadows from the frozen lumps of earth on the road
toward him. Then it had gone, and it was immediately
almost completely dark, with not a star, not a sound.

But the road was bordered by hedges which helped
him keep his direction. Once he thought he heard
loud breathing across the hedge and he stood still.
Could a horse or a cow have been left outside in a
winter night? He waited motionless but the sound did
not recur; then he went on, almost running now, for he
was afraid. It was much later when he saw a little
light, an oil lamp behind a window, and came to the
farmhouse he had been aiming for.

It took awhile before the farmer understood and
believed that A. had been with those campers who
used to help bring in his hay. A. remembered all the
names, of the wife, the son, the daughters, the helpers,
and finally the old man let a smile appear on his face.
"Oh yes," he mumbled, "those boys from the city."
They were at their evening meal: the man and his
wife, and two haggard and already used-up looking
girls—the daughters who had that summer, long ago,
seemed so sunny and vivacious and strong. There was
a pan with soup in the middle of the table, and they
had all poured some in their bowls. A. brought his
bread and cheese out and made a gesture for them to
help themselves from it. One of the girls picked up the
cheese, then put it down again. No one ate.

"And now what?" the farmer asked. "Have you
come to help with the hay again? You're a bit late in
the year."

The girls laughed, covering their mouths with their
hands. A. laughed too.

"You've got that field near the border," he said, "I remember, with the barn at the edge of the wood." He gave a push against the botany kit and let it swing on the strap over the back of his chair. "I'm a university student now, and I am writing about coniferae, that is, pine trees, some rare kinds which grow up here. I want to spend the night there if I may. I won't make a fire, you can lend me some straw, or a blanket maybe. I have to make my observations very early in the morning."

While he talked, the family had started eating their soup, all at the same time, and now the farmer put his spoon down without looking up. He looked painfully embarrassed. Why? A. wondered, because he's going to say no?

Then he realized the farmer was embarrassed not for his own sake, but for him because he knew A. was lying.

No one answered him.

"Hell, no, that's not the reason," A. then said. "I have to smuggle a friend across the border."

The wife got up and brought him a bowl. "It's not much of a soup for city people," she said, "but it's warm."

The farmer ate some soup, cleared his throat, and then said so loudly that it surprised everyone, "Our government is not men, it is birds of prey. And that's unjust to birds, who only do as nature tells them. Our government eats blood." He waited, looking at each of them in turn, and then went on, "That field was taken away from me long ago. By the military. With a paper. A year later there was a letter. I should go to the city and get my money for it. A hundred and twelve francs. That same month they drafted my son into the army. He hasn't written in three months now. I—" He stopped that sentence. "That hay—you know how much we got in all, this year? Five cartloads. Five."

"Five," A. repeated, not knowing what else to comment on that.

"Our son's all right," the wife said. "I can feel it. I often dream about him."

A. pushed the bread and cheese across the table. The farmer cut off small pieces, which he held out to them on the point of his knife.

"You can sleep here," he said, "and before it gets light one of my daughters can take you across. They know the way."

XVIII

A. SLEPT in a blanket in front of the stove, but when he was awakened, the air was so stone-cold that it hurt to breathe.

The older daughter was blowing on the coals. She turned and nodded at him. "I'm making chicory for us," she said, "to warm up."

"Are you sure it's safe to go—for you, I mean?" A. whispered.

"You don't have to whisper. Everyone's awake. It's my third crossing this year. Mary has done four. That's half what we live on now, taking stuff across."

Outside the air was still and the cold less numbing than A. had thought. There was some ragged light now and then from a waning moon.

They walked beside each other. "You can hold on to my cape," the girl said, "it's rough ground."

After a while she whispered. "Now you better stay behind me. There's soldiers here, sometimes."

He followed her silhouette which was not much more than a greater blackness in the dark around him. He stumbled but hastened on, touching her cape to make sure he was behind her. Then she stood still, and he stood beside her, catching his breath. "Look," she said.

He stared and blinked, trying to sort out real dark and light from the flickering behind his eyes. He made out a vague glimmer ahead, crossing their road, a trail which collected a diffused bit of light.

"It's the sand path," she said. "That's the border."

"Oh."

"You can't see it now, but to the right of us, a hundred feet only, is our old barn. I think it's empty. If you go straight ahead, you come to the other one. That one's across the border, of course. The river is down there, to the right. There's only one train a day going across. At half past seven. It'll be light then. I'll wait with you here till you can see where you're going."

"No, I don't want that," A. whispered urgently, "really not. I know where I am. I'll walk around here under this tree, keep myself warm. You go home. And thank you, thank you very much."

"Are you sure?" the girl asked.

"Yes."

But she did not leave yet; he could feel the warmth of her body more than see her.

"That man you're smuggling across," she then began.

"Yes?"

"Do you mind my asking?"

He shook his head in the dark, then said, "No, I don't."

"Is he coming here, or is he escaping from here?"

"He's coming here."

"Yes, that's what we figured; otherwise he would have been with you, wouldn't he? We also figured he has to be important—I mean for a gentleman from the city to come here for him. Is he?"

"Yes," A. said. "You don't know how grateful we are to you, and to your father."

"Oh, that's not what I mean," the girl said almost impatiently. "What we want to ask—is he so important that he has the power—I mean, will he change things? Will things change?"

A. swallowed. He thought he could see her light

eyes then, but he wasn't sure he was not just imagining it. "Oh, I hope so," he finally answered, "I hope so."

XIX

HE STOOD under a tree, shivering, and watched the sun rise through the pine trees and light up the barren fields. How were those words in Dostoevski, he thought, about, why are the fields so naked, why are people so poor?

But why do I have to think of that; why do we nurse those literary feelings and indignations? Why do we need reading about it? I can just plunge my hands into the earth, like this, like this, and that is how men live, nine out of ten men and women.

But *of course* it cannot go on. It is totally self-explanatory that it cannot. How could it be questionable and debatable, why do we need theories?

He had actually plunged his hands into the ground, and as he straightened up, he heard the whistle of the train and saw its white smoke above the horizon.

He took a deep breath and shook his head as if to clear it that way. I got a bit hysterical there, he thought, wiping his hands on his coat, and he tried to shake the earth out from under his bleeding nails. Then he crossed the sand trail and half ran, half walked, to the barn in the distance, which stood in an empty field and was eminently visible, struck by the rising sun. Not a very suitable place we picked for our rendezvous, he said to himself. He stopped and decided to stay in the bushes which came within a few hundred yards of it. Not a sound was heard. Perhaps they gave him his breakfast first, sometimes soldiers and police show that kind of crooked good-fellowship. Perhaps they wait till it's dark. God, that would be awful, sitting here all day. I hope Wenster would have the sense to say he'd rather cross right away.

He found that he hadn't been thinking of Wenster at all, neither the preceding day nor now; they were all assuming he was doing this great deed of solidarity and he hadn't given the man a thought. Wenster was just an alibi, no, not that, a chance to be—he didn't know what. I'll tell him immediately, though, he decided, I don't want to be thanked by him, there'll be no phoniness about it. Just a job, Wenster.

Very indistinctly he heard something; he couldn't define it but felt it was an unpleasant noise; then it became clearer; it was the barking of dogs.

"Oh damn, damn," he said aloud, "I hate that." If they patrolled along the frontier with dogs, they'd catch him. He stood up straight, saw nothing, and without further waiting, ran to the barn.

It had no door, it was dark and empty, and in spite of the cold it was penetrated by a foul smell. There were some low wooden beams across the floor, and scraps of paper were blowing about. It had been used as a latrine—by the northern border patrols, he assumed. He shrugged. Damn you, Wenster, he thought. No, that's not fair. He installed himself in the southeast corner of the structure, huddled in his coat, and peered through the cracks between the planks. He could see a helmet now; a soldier with two German shepherd dogs was walking along the trail. They were huge dogs, but the soldier looked half asleep and not very frightening; he let himself be more or less dragged along. They passed the place where A. had crossed, but nothing happened. The dogs barked as before but continued westward, and then the team vanished out of sight behind the bushes.

He wiped his face. A sharp wind was blowing through the cracks, but there was nothing in the barn to make any kind of shelter with. He stamped his feet and beat his arms, and stopped thinking about the cold.

XX

BEYOND the empty strip along all frontiers lie the fields, the frozen or the burning earth, caked, soaked, and the people bending from morning till night, turning their backs blindly toward the sky, forcing out the food for others to eat. Or they bend over benches and wheels, identically, with man-made heat and cold, steam and sulphur for rain and wind, still peasants. They still carry us and we are as far from life as a man in a litter is from the surface of the road; floating, he not even ignores, he not-knows it.

We must stand up at last, and dry the tears of humanity, those centuries of tears. Here is this country tilting its surface toward the sun, and the men in the offices and the palaces and the streets quite shamelessly reveal what they have done with their patrimony, how they have despoiled it and put in an iron vice; by what magic do they live and see without seeing all this weariness?

And the dead pseudo-soldier, the son of my farmer, born in a dirty bed, fed on pig scraps, sent out to work as soon as he was old enough to laugh, brought to the town, read into the army with their voodoo rite, gone to her room with a street girl on his last leave, his first and only woman, the only time he felt himself coming in a girl who stared at the ceiling and then jumped up and went to wash from a basin at the window, now he is dead and rotting and eaten, disintegrating in the mud.

He was outside the world in this barn, a no man's land from where he could watch and judge and not be judged. As the sun reached the door opening, he shifted with the square of light it projected in which there was some warmth, and he was linked to it that way, and the earth turned under him without him. He had that feeling again that all was possible, even to him, but this time it did not make him happy.

It was night, there was a black freezing sky with stars blazing at him; and Wenster had not come. He left the barn; as he came out he was knocked against the wall by the wind which had risen in strength all through the day; he started walking.

When he had come within sight of the lighted window of his farm once more, he realized that he couldn't knock on their door. He had forced himself to wait all day in the barn on the theory that they might indeed deport people after dark only, but he had thought of making it just back to the farm. He had made his way there, thinking of nothing but their fire and their soup, and had not thought that if he showed up like this, they would know the plan had not worked.

"Will things change?" he said softly, imitating the cadence in the girl's voice. It would be too much, facing them like that, I couldn't bear it.

He went on, forcing himself not to look back at their lamp, moving as if he were wading through sand or water rather than walking.

When he came to the railway junction, he thought if someone questioned him now he would just burst into tears; he couldn't speak or think any more. But all was in darkness, there was no one there. He walked up to the shed where he had seen the rural guard the day before. Its door was locked, but on the impetus of those last twenty–four hours he kicked it open in one movement, without deliberating. The potbellied stove inside was still warm.

XXI

A. GOT BACK to his building at noon of the following day. The door to his room was ajar, it was thick with tobacco smoke in there; they had obviously been sitting around waiting for him. There was a note from Anne on the table, "Welcome back! We hope it did all go well, you are our hero! We've just gone over to Lacanau's place for a meeting. Come there, or wait for me here, please. I won't be gone long." A meeting, he said to himself, looking in the mirror which stood on the mantelpiece, another meeting. He sat down on the bed (Anne had bought it at an auction for twelve francs, out of his mother's money present), took off his shoes and started rubbing his feet.

As he opened his eyes, Anne was leaning over him and she brushed the hair out of his face. The room was full of people. "I'm sorry," he muttered with a dry throat, "I must have fallen asleep."

Anne sat down beside him and put her hand on his arm. "Poor man," she said, "you are exhausted. I'll take care of you."

They were standing around him now and looking at him; finally the professor asked, "Did you take Wenster to his hideout?"

He shook his head. "Wenster never came. I waited twelve hours."

They all started speaking. "That's rotten news," the professor said. "We have heard from our contact that he is no longer in the Delta Prison. . . . Are you all right? Was there any danger?"

A. shrugged with a gesture not of indifference but of resignation.

"You must tell us about it. You've done more than your share anyway. We are very proud of you in the committee."

"They talked about nothing but you in Lacanau's room," Anne whispered in his ear.

A. stood up and went to the window. "I'm quitting," he told them.

"You are not," one of the students half asked, half ordered him.

"He's tired and disheartened," the professor said to them in the gently pedagogic voice he could assume, "and that shouldn't surprise us. He'll feel better tomorrow."

"Perhaps we should leave him in peace for a bit," Lacanau said. He went over to A. and shook his hand. "We're still appreciative, very much so. You tried."

There was a general leave-taking, while Anne rummaged in his closet and fished out a pair of socks, of different colors but without holes. As they all walked out, A. stood in the doorway.

"I'm *not* disheartened," he said hesitantly.

The last man to leave turned around, and some others, already on the staircase, stopped too.

"It's just the opposite," A. went on, hurrying his words. "It's that we take too much time. And we get hurt just the same. There isn't that much time. And what's more, we're hypocrites. We don't submit to the men in power, and we don't hold them up with a pistol. We say, please sirs, surrender just a little out of your wallet. Why would they? Why the hell would they? Surely nobody ever, ever, voluntarily surrendered power? Look at America, four years of war before the slave owners—and even so—"

By now half the committee members were back on the landing, and the professor said, "The serfs in Russia were set free by the Czar without any war."

"They were almost worse off afterward," A. said, "with the land owners making more money out of them and their land than ever. Didn't you tell us that once yourself? Didn't you write somewhere that the French Revolution was stopped in its tracks by just one group of people, a hundred thousand fat burghers, when *they* had got what they wanted?"

The professor smiled. "It's a pity you're not one of my students, they refuse to remember what I proved to them a week before," he said. "But I never called anyone a fat burgher."

A. smiled back at him. "I know this is all just café talk," he said. "It's really, in the end, only a matter of what you feel."

"Well?" someone asked, "So what? What are you going to do about it?"

"I'm going over to the others," A. said. "I'm going to be the agitator the police commissioner thinks I am anyway."

"Oh no," Anne said beside him, taking his hand.

He went back into the room with her. She let go of his hand, and he sat down and started putting on his dry socks.

She looked at him and took a deep breath. "If you go over to them," she then announced, "I will too."

"I don't want you to," A. answered in a low voice. "I have to do this alone."

Anne started to cry.

XXII

To go and see the others, he should first look the way he did when he was still living at home; they shouldn't think like that café owner that he was dressing a part. He had the idea of asking Anne to go to his house and try to get hold of some of his things left behind there. They went together; he waited around the corner to be out of sight. She reappeared with a suitcase, and looking pleased with herself. His mother was back, she told him, and encouraged by Anne's presence, had packed it with her. They had had a nice talk, and Anne had promised her help to get the two together. His mother was in great fear that A.'s father would hear about such meetings.

"Your father must be an ogre," Anne said.

"Oh, he's sacrificing his love to his principles. He's finding it surprisingly painless too, I think."

"I told your mother you had quit our committee," Anne said. "She asked me about my work in it, and it came out before I could decide if you wanted her to know."

"It makes no difference."

And so the following day a note from his father was delivered to A. in his room, in which he expressed his pleasure with A.'s breaking with the Radicals and announced that his house was once more open to him; the regrettable intermezzo was forgotten. A. sat down to write a humorous answer that he had left the Radicals only because they were unradical, but it didn't turn out very funny and he decided to leave his father's letter unanswered.

He set his hopes on a fellow student, a man older than the others, who had been arrested a year earlier and finally released and even readmitted to the university upon a promise to abstain from all political activity. A. knew him only by sight, and to get hold of him he had to wait for classes to start. After the first seminar in the new year he went over to him and asked his help, but the man immediately walked away.

A. kept up beside him. "You haven't asked what I'd need your help for," he said.

"It makes no difference. There's nothing I could or want to help anyone with. Unless it's a mechanical matter, like carrying a box of books. But then you shouldn't have picked me, I am surely not the strongest of our class."

"Give me ten minutes," A. answered, "and then decide."

The man sighed.

He sat down on a stone bench in the little square in front of the main auditorium. It was a pleasant spot on a summer's day, but not in the eddy of ice-cold winds blowing around the buildings. "Ten minutes, then," he said. He crossed his legs and indicated he was waiting.

Dust blew in their faces. A. began to laugh. "I'll make it five," he said, clutching his scarf. "I was on the Radical Party committee."

"Was?"

"I quit because—"

"Don't tell me. I don't want to know."

"I want to work more—more for real; I'm tired of being an amateur. But I don't want to stir up things by going around asking questions. I'd like to go straight to the center."

"And you think I'd give you the name of a man to see? I haven't spoken those names, not after three months solitary, and in a very narrow cell, I can tell you."

"Yes, I've heard about that," A. said.

"Then what makes you think I'd toss them off to you on a bench here?"

A. shrugged. "I want to help, if they'll have me."

"Why do you want to help them? You think that it would be exciting? That it would make you happy?"

"I—" A. began.

"Think it over before you answer."

"I don't think at all it would make me happy. My happiness is not my object in life. But of course I am happy realizing just that."

The man made a face and sighed again. Then he stood up, and A. thought he would leave him there without another answer; but instead he crossed his arms in a touchingly archaic gesture, as if to indicate his resignation to living in a world of fools, and said, "You can go and see Despard. He works in the National Iron Foundry, in the designing room. But don't barge in there and tackle him the way you did me."

"Do you think—" A. said, but the man had already turned around and marched off, his head bent down against the wind.

XXIII

A. WAS LYING in his twelve-franc bed which he thought wasn't actually more comfortable than his straw mattress, and stared at the ceiling of his room. It was a light night, for fresh snow had fallen in the streets and the reflected moonlight drew strange patterns on his ceiling, of unexplainable regularity. The little stove had gone out and he could see his breath. Beside him, with her back turned, Anne was asleep curled up, her hands between her legs. She had wanted to stay the night; she was wearing two old sweaters of his, one over the other. He could feel her cold bottom against his right leg. He was not thinking properly; images moved through his head and he observed them without much acuteness. Earlier, when Anne was lying with her head on his shoulder, she had suddenly said, "You know, it's very difficult what you're going to do and brave. They're all arguing about it with you, but I wonder how many of us would have the nerve to go really illegal." He had not answered.

And then he had begun wondering if he himself had the nerve; if he wanted it; if it were really necessary in life always to do the hardest thing.

Seventeen, he was just admitted as a freshman to

one of the fraternities; a black beret with a yellow edge, yellow for the faculty of philosophy. They were sitting at the window of the fraternity house, drinking beer, and when girls walked by and curiously looked inside, they pretended not to notice.

He was in a fencing class—how sweet life appeared when you walked along the streets in the late fall afternoon, the light shining in the rainy pavements, carrying a foil and a fencing glove, people staring a bit. Waking up in the morning very late, after a party, decide to skip class and sit in a café, everyone else working, leaf through magazines, smoke, liking everything and yourself.

The National Library, the manuscript room which had been such a mysterious place to him when he was in high school and not allowed in there—now here he was, showing his pass, the old assistant unlocking the little gate and taking him to his seat, coming back later with his books which he placed in front of him with a little bow; the old men here and there in the room, a few students, one very fierce-looking young woman—their eyes rested on him and moved on, his presence was accepted, he belonged, and old, rare books yielded to his hands.

A Sunday afternoon at home, the silence seeping in from the street. *The People,* folded by his father at the editorial page, some remarks underlined—not in horror, but in approval, the nauseating hypocrisy of these people, the *unjustness* of their explaining ideas falsely and then attacking them, attacking their own chimeras. It was a feeling now mixed with the smell of the Sunday dinner brought in, little game birds in a ring of potatoes with berries. Perhaps he had joined the Radical Party because his father was talking to him about the president and he was half listening and staring at the severed joint of a slightly underdone bird on his plate, the little red veins in the tissue visible through the drops of sauce.

Then came this building, this room on warm evenings, the window propped open, Anne, whom he'd just met, coming in breathlessly, for she always ran up all the stairs, with a newsletter from abroad, or a student pamphlet, or a cake she had stolen for him during a visit with some relative; the sound of the dripping tap on the landing, voices from the street; an almost-nostalgia, an almost-real scene from the life of a bohemian student, The Student Rebel, operetta in five acts and an epilogue.

He saw a ball in an unknown city, a dazzling room, candles; he was an attaché-of-embassy and danced with Helen Peret, touched the cool curve of her back, they stepped out onto the terrace under a subtropical sky, glasses were brought, of champagne of course. Then he changed the evening clothes for the old jacket he had worn at the border to find Wenster; now he was in that garden after climbing through a hedge; Helen was on the terrace with someone else, but she was distracted and stared beyond her escort; he whistled softly and she saw him, pointed furtively to a little Chinese tea pavilion in the middle of the pond—

Then the dirty, windy alley beside the police station, and suddenly some policemen dragging him out of that side door, limp and bleeding; they opened a garbage can and pushed him in, they couldn't get the lid on and one of them stepped on his head, something snapped, they snickered, and the lid fitted. "God, no," he whispered before he fell asleep.

XXIV

GOING DOWN the long corridor of the mathematical institute of the university, with its peeling plaster and old green paint on the walls, A. became aware of a girl standing near the far exit door, her back toward the light. It's Helen, he said to himself, no, it can't be. I hope it isn't. Has she seen me? He let some people pass him and then turned around and went back into the empty classroom.

She can't be here for me. So why not walk past her and say hello? It would be interesting to see how she reacts.

Now he half hoped she was waiting to see him; he had told her he was a student of Professor Saitzew. He quickly went out. She was still there; and as he came up to her, he produced something between a nod and a bow. She said good morning in a tone of voice which made him stand still. She was a marvelous appearance in the dingy vestibule, he thought, all in fur, with a fur hat, her face framed in its softness. She blushed slightly. "You shouldn't misunderstand my coming here," she said. "I was angry with myself, for acting so—so like outraged virtue. I was rude."

It took A. a moment to understand that she was there for him and had never expected him not to think so.

"But not at all," A. answered, "I don't know now how I could have behaved so preposterously." And on an impulse he went on, "You see, I realized I would never meet someone like you socially. I mean, I'd never be introduced anyway and so I had nothing to lose."

She gave him a friendly smile. "That's why I have come to apologize. I don't want you to feel I acted the way I did because, because—"

"Because I'm poor," A. finished.

She started looking at his clothes but stopped herself; then she shrugged and made a face, very childishly.

"But we can't stand here," A. said. "Would you come and have some tea with me somewhere?"

"Oh no, no, I can't, I am on my way to an appointment. You must excuse me now."

"Yes," A. said.

He was taken aback. She had spoiled something by

coming there, by not at all being as unapproachable as he had made her; but she must have thought from his face he felt rejected, probably once more because of his shabby appearance, and she added, "You can write to me if you want to," and vanished through the door.

A. began to laugh. Write to her. "You've got a nerve," he said loudly to the closed door and kicked it, which made a flake of paint come off.

The porter came out of his booth and told him, "I have to take your name for that."

XXV

WHEN he came outside, she had gone. Only some students were walking up and down in the pale sunlight. He turned right, crossed the square, and started up the long avenue to the suburb where the foundry stood and which was drearily named Irontown.

He had promised himself to think about it some more before going to see Despard, but now it seemed that he should go immediately. Perhaps it was the strange visit of Helen Peret that morning which made him feel it was unseemly to wait. As he followed the avenue he no longer reconsidered; he was going through with it.

There was hardly any traffic on the wide, straight road—built that way, it was believed, to provide a good field of fire against any demonstrators from the industrial sections marching toward the center of town. Gradually its character changed; the trees disappeared, empty lots were strewn with rubbish, fences covered with torn posters. There was a level crossing of the western railway line, and beyond that the brick houses ended, giving way to wooden shacks and workshops, with here and there still a little farm, caught in the outflow of the town, chickens, a skinny cow looking dirty under the dark sky. The factories were near and the air was smudged by them. Rows of industrial housing began lining the avenue which slowly climbed here, miserable little houses, one against the other, making a staircase of humanity. Some of them, however, were not joined but incomprehensibly built just a few inches apart, leaving a gap too narrow to enter, filling up through time with unmentionable debris. There were yards in which people kept the coal they bought from the factory; hedges and plants were struggling for survival, everything covered with a black film of coal dust. It became livelier: women were hanging up laundry, talking to each other, shouting at children, night-shift factory workers were seen sitting in their kitchens or tinkering in their yards; boys were running errands. Children stopped and stared at A. as he walked by; but most adults ignored him or, he thought, studiously turned their backs.

He was sitting across from Despard in a storage space next to the designing room which the men used for eating their bread at noon. Despard was drinking cold black coffee from a tin cup. He asked, "So you're bringing me greetings from my brother. How are things in my old town?"

"Fine," A. said. "Or perhaps not so fine. The winter is always tough there. You know."

Despard did not answer, but as he put his cup down on a stack of planks, he pointed back with his thumb toward a corner, where a man was sitting, picking his teeth, not looking in their direction.

Someone came over to Despard, put a hand on his shoulder, and asked, "How about a quick beer across the road?"

Despard stood up, and A. too; he expected to be asked along. But Despard turned away and only said to him, "Well, thanks again for the message," as he followed the man out. Now all the others looked at A., who reddened and hastily left. As he walked toward the gate, he saw Despard and his friend crossing the open space in front of the factory and he slowed his step to avoid catching up with them. Then he was out on the avenue again, faced with another three-mile walk back to town. "Damn that man," he muttered, "what does he think he's doing?" A cart appeared from behind the factory wall, pulled by a team of heavy draft horses. It was not loaded; two boys were sitting on an upturned crate in the back. On the avenue it turned toward town. A. waved his hand at the driver to ask for a ride, and the cart slowed down, he thought. He ran toward it but it did not stop, and as it passed him, one of the boys scooped up a handful of sawdust and threw it at him, which made them all laugh. The other boy did a little dance step which caused him almost to fall off and cried at A., "I say, what's the matter, sir? Didn't your carriage wait for you?" "Drop dead you bastards," A. shouted back, which created a new chorus of laughs.

To hell with them all, A. thought, I've done my best now, I'll wash my hands of the whole damn business, go back home and tell my father he was right and bring out the fatted calf. Go and call on Helen, black tie, an apostatizing Kropotkin, the beggar prince.

He stood in the road, trying to brush the sawdust out of his collar. Two passing women stared at him and he asked them, "Anything I can do for you?" Why don't these people realize I'm on their side?

But that is a senseless and even vile question. For there's only the side of injustice and the side of justice. Goddammit, it's really that simple, and if it isn't, we have to declare it is. And the fence runs pretty much between rich and poor, bank accounts and pawnshop tickets, pink hands and dirty hands. And only because I was born on the wrong, the unjust side of the fence, have I learned to call it justice, and am not quite comfortable when they simply call it, food. Why, for chrissake then, should they be nice? I'm not doing them any favor. And they're not doing me any.

There are so many armies in this great invisible war—it's up to me, to anybody, to find out where you belong. If you want to. And then join it, try to join it.

I hadn't thought, I was too preoccupied with my own fears and reservations. I hadn't admitted it to myself, but I had half expected some great welcome, how noble of you, brother, to come down to us, to give up all those marvelous privileges your father's money could get you. That was no revolutionary walk I made this morning along this road; I was just a frilly lady taking a pot of soup to the *deserving* poor, filled to her neck with self-righteous love for herself and for her love-for-others, I was going to make my little contribution toward helping them. But what I'm after is helping myself, freeing myself.

Back to Despard. I must get through to him.

He turned around and started back up the road to the factory.

XXVI

A TIME of limbo followed. He had succeeded in getting himself interviewed one evening by Despard and another man whose name was never mentioned, and been told to wait. They were afraid of informers and police infiltrators; weeks went by without a word from them. And now the members of the Radical committee didn't come to his room any more, and he found of course that he missed them. Anne made appearances, but always in a hurry to be off somewhere for the committee; "It isn't that important, is it?" he would ask, and she answered, "Yes, it just so happens that it is," and he, "Well, things must have changed since my days." She would shrug, and then suddenly look so fragile and vulnerable that he hastened to comfort her and to tell her that of course it was important, and that he was being unpleasant because he was jealous, which was not true. There were occasions when he realized she was willing to stay and make love, and he pretended not to understand and let the chance pass by—he felt guilty toward her and it helped when he abstained from "using" her as much as he might have. The committee seemed a bit silly to him, but he had also lost some of his awe for the others, for Despard and the men of the Second International Association. There had been something so splendid, triumphant almost, for him in that very word international, conjuring up the final true brotherhood; the first reality of Despard and his friend had been jarring. A petty reaction though.

Once a week his mother fed him an enormous lunch, but he refused to accept further money from her, for she had to account for every penny. "Why do you make life so difficult for yourself?" she asked without fail. "Why do you fight things so? Nobody is going to thank you for it." Although he was much alone, he had less spare time, for he had found outside work to keep him going awhile: making an index to a vast study on Marco Polo. It was very badly paid of course, and it was deadeningly boring. His hours, formerly filled with all their deliberations and discussions, silently and endlessly spent over the manuscript with its footnotes in every language—he wore half his wardrobe against the cold, put out his supper of bread and sausage or cheese or just tomato paste on the mantelpiece, to be eaten when he became really desperate to get out of his chair and move; and a strong underlying feeling of waste, of missing out, and being alive and young to no purpose.

He was sitting in his room as close as possible to the window, stacks of manuscript on one side, dictionaries from the library beside his chair, and all the various boxes with cards in front of him. He had to look for a name in one sheaf of papers; half of them slipped out of the binding; a card had been put under the wrong letter and refused to be found; his pen fell first on his trousers, then on the floor. His hands were trembling with frustration; if he had had a public, if Anne had been sitting in a corner and pitying him, he would have thrown all those cards through the room. There was little point however in doing that while he was alone, and then having to pick them up again himself.

Thus in the early evening, staring at the corner of sky he could see, the purple clouds of the freezing sunset, his stove smoking, he turned over a card on which he was about to make an entry, and began writing a letter on it instead.

Helen, I cannot get your face, the image of you, out of my mind—as you were standing in your fur coat in the lobby of the institute—(that's even true in a way, he thought). A penniless student doesn't perhaps fit in your world, but that feeling is so strong that it is worthy of you—

She won't take that seriously. Yes, she will.

He couldn't think of anything else to add. He had the feeling that he could not stay in his room another minute. He put the card to Helen in his pocket, peeled off two of the three pairs of socks he was wearing against the cold, put his shoes on and his coat.

He hastened through the silent streets, through the pale air, to the center of town. How easy it was to cut off the links one had, to be reduced to zero; he had made no dent on the world and would vanish unnoticed if he died now.

He entered the Crystal Café where he had not set foot for months, and saw old student friends of his at several tables. To his pleasure, they welcomed him with some excitement. He smiled mysteriously when asked where he had been hiding all that time. They made him sit down with them; the owner came over and A. told him in a whisper that he had made up with his father and would within a few days straighten out his bill. In the meantime, he would pay cash of course. The story fitted well with his own mood and he was believed; the café owner sent over a brandy in honor of his return. Beers were passed on to him from several tables, and he sat there happily and realizing with some smugness that the conversation had not changed, that in fact the topics seemed to

consist of the very same little incidents, jokes, and
melodramas of a year ago. Then the talk turned to
women and love. A. pulled the card out of his pocket
and added in a scribble, "Please meet me tonight at
the Crystal Café, it is terribly important." He asked
for an envelope at the buffet, addressed it, and gave
ten francs to an apprentice waiter to deliver it immediately. That tip, seen by several of his friends and
by the café owner, made a considerable impression.

He should bow out at his zenith, A. thought, and he
announced, "I'm expecting someone," and installed
himself in a corner of the room, next to the heavy
purple curtains covering the doors to the dining room.
The warmth of the café, and perhaps also the fact that
he had not eaten, made his head swim, and he took a
measure of pride in his own realization that he didn't
precisely know what he was doing.

XXVII

AN HOUR LATER, regrettably just after his friends had
left, Helen came in. She was wearing a sort of travel
coat with a hood in which she tried to hide her face;
she stood rigidly at the door, afraid to look around,
saw him, quickly came over, and sat down with her
back to the room. A. stood up and sat down again.

"I can only stay a minute," the girl said. "I've never been in a place like this."

"I'm very grateful," A. said.

"I didn't want to let you down . . ." She hesitated. "Why did you say it was so important?"

"Because I can't work. I have to prepare for my exam, and all I can think of is you."

She smiled, then she made a face. "You must forget our—everything."

"Very well, I will," A. answered.

She stood up. A. followed her example.

"Have a beer," he suggested.

"A beer? I have to go."

"When can I see you again? You must agree to see me. All this is not my fault; I had pulled myself together, and then you suddenly showed up again."

She looked uncertainly at him. "I'm giving a party for my friends next Sunday," she then said. "If you want to come . . . I'll tell my parents I met you at Lydia's house."

"Who is Lydia?"

She did not answer, and he thought she was already sorry for her invitation.

"Well, no," he said, "I wouldn't fit in, I don't want to come to a party. I want to be alone with you."

"Without my parents knowing you?" she asked.

Oh, for God's sake, he thought. He felt the euphoria of the evening run out of him. I'm just making a complete fool of myself.

XXVIII

IN THE pitch-black evening A. was going down a street from door to door.

He had been accepted by the others. There had been strong opposition because he was a student, and he had offered to try and get a job, any job, at the foundry, but he had been assured that would be impossible; they were laying off men.

Finally, with considerable solemnity, he had been told what their project was, the one he should work on: a general strike in the town.

Because of the foremen it was almost impossible to make propaganda in the factories. Instead they called on the people in their houses, after the night shift and after the day shift. It was tricky work. Despard had said to him, "I quote you Proudhon: the greatest obstacle that equality has to overcome is not the aristocratic pride of the rich but the undisciplined egoism of the poor." A. had looked at him and Despard had laughed; it had been the only occasion any of them had been sententious. But now A. found some pleasure in repeating softly to himself, "undisciplined egoism," as doors were shut in his face, pamphlets thrown back out after him, and once as he had to slither down a muddy alley, attacked by a dog which the owner obviously was in no hurry to call off. Were they just afraid, did they think he was an agent provocateur? He lacked the experience to guess and the patience to broach the object of his visits in a roundabout way.

One woman let him in, motioning him to speak softly because the children were sleeping. She was a widow; all of them worked, she told him. "What will we live on if we join your strike?" she asked. "You don't have to join any strike," A. answered, "not now. You join our organization, and after that all we do is by joint decision and joint action. If there's a strike, everyone will help everyone."

"Like when my husband was killed," she said. "I got seven francs the first week, then three, then nothing."

"This is different; it's going to be very different."

"Is it all right to join?" she asked.

"You mean is it legal? Is it legal to starve? Is it legal for them to live off the work of others? To send us to wars for them, against men like ourselves? We must fight for our rights, nobody will give them to us for free."

She sighed. "But when they find out, I'll be fired, won't I? You have nothing to worry about—I can tell from your hands you don't work." She said those words with a little smile as if to show they were not meant bitterly.

A. shrugged. He tried to wiggle his feet, which were very wet, within his shoes.

They were silent. The woman turned the lamp low, to save oil obviously; the vast shadows climbed over the walls and the ceiling. "I work in my own way," A. finally said. "We're all in this. If you go skating and one man falls through the ice, he won't insist the others fall through too before he'll let them help him . . . There's no division of interest on our side of the fence. It's precisely the men on top of us who'd like you to think that."

She looked past him, still with her vague smile. "I used to go skating as a young girl," she announced.

A. laughed, and stood up. "Well, thank you for listening anyway," he answered. "That's more than most do."

"Wait," she said. She took a jar from a shelf and fished out some coins. "Here's my money for one month. I join." He thanked her; it was his first success.

XXIX

THERE WAS less fraternity, less common feeling in it all than A. had expected. These men went neither through the spells of euphoria the Radical committee knew, nor through its moods of frustration and futility; they pursued their course solidly, perhaps stolidly. Most of them did not smoke or drink, every penny went toward the work, and Despard's beers were not smiled upon. The ideas moving them were taken for granted; there was little debate on theory, and occasional phrases or speech-making were quickly smothered. Their organization was outlawed, as they knew by experience only, for the government had never even mentioned its existence. Thus their aversion to meetings had very practical justification. Everyone worked more or less on his own, usually contacting only one other man; A. did not get to know any of them well except Despard himself. After a while he met a few others, when he was asked to help in their only common work: a kind of school they ran, "emancipation classes" in someone or other's room where a few workmen came to listen to talks or just to learn reading and writing. He became aware of divisions and tensions, men who avoided each other or whispered in corners, but remained outside all that. A. knew they had one or two underground presses working in the city, but he only saw the pamphlets given to him to use on his visits. I'd like to take my father along just once, he thought, to see these puritanical and grim men who study political economy and who refuse a beer; he imagines them as debauched wild agitators. Despard had told A. to dress like a workman, which was very unlike being dressed like a poor student, and he had lent A. the clothes for it. For this rather small town (as capitals go) actually consisted of two towns, divided by an unsurmountable wall, and a student seen in the workingmen's quarters stood out as much as a workman in a restaurant on Main Avenue. Both aroused suspicion, both would soon be followed by police agents.

But on some occasions, precisely because of A.'s background—"That bourgeois liberal face of yours," Despard said—he was asked to act under his own colors, to be a student and call on little shopkeepers and such, people who could have made important allies. Each time it was a catastrophe; he was stared at in astonishment, threatened with a beating, and in one dingy workshop a shoemaker grabbed him and yelled for his wife to get the police; A. had to hit the man in his face to free himself and escape. Here he got the full stream of abuse, the remarks his father used to paraphrase in nicer words, you're all atheist materialists, dirty foreigners, antichrists, terrorists, dirty jews. "Materialists? Because we demand a minimum, one-tenth of what the rich take completely for granted in life?" A. had asked the shoemaker. "And they're less materialistic because they work up an appetite for their Sunday dinner in church?" That was when the man had started screaming "Antichrists! You shot the archbishop of Paris!" and taken hold of his arms.

A. often confessed to himself that he didn't have enough physical courage; as a boy he was always cowed by his classmates. The shoemaker was not a big man, but he had the unthinking aggressiveness which paralyzed A. They grappled, stumbling against things; the shoemaker picked up an awl. It was the smell of his body that freed A., you poor slob, he thought, who do you think you're defending, you stink, they wouldn't even let you in at the kitchen door. He struck the man in his face, and ran off; the wife was shouting in the street.

But even with the most miserable factory workers there was some of that, an astonishing mentality, from centuries of being at the bottom, he thought, an idea that there was something unnatural and not right in rebelling, in standing up, something "international," they said. "But international is not a dirty word," A. answered, "it's a beautiful word, a Christian word if you want. It means we finally recognize common humanity, we are no longer fooled by presidents and kings and rulers and the myths of flags and history and hatred for our neighbors." "Are you from this country?" he would be asked suspiciously. "Yes, don't I sound it?" "Sure, but . . ."

Slowly he learned to omit all that, except when talking to very young people. He learned to sound like the man who went around selling funeral insurance at five francs a year, very businesslike, very daily. In fact, his best ploy became one where he started out talking about funeral insurance, which usually created interest—equally with those who did not have it and with those who did, and wondered if they paid too much. Then he would say, "What we want you to sign up for may do you some good before you're dead." Said in the right tone of voice, that would make them laugh.

He also learned to say matter-of-factly, "It's a very

short form, shall I just fill it out for you?" For there
were some who had refused to join because they could
not write and did not want to admit that.

And thus a few signed up, to perhaps strike one day
if the word was given, perhaps one day come out into
the open for the first time and count themselves. To
A., walking home with his pamphlets under his coat, a
handful of pennies' contributions in his pocket, and
the Marco Polo manuscript waiting for him in his
room, it seemed very far off.

XXX

WAKING UP that Sunday, he could tell from the bright
light that it was late, probably past noon already; the
corridor and the house were silent. He had got home
at two or three in the morning after a strange expedi-
tion. Despard had taken him from café to café in the
eastern suburb at the other end of the town where
they did not know him, talking everywhere to the men
who, with their payday money in their pockets, were
crowding around the bars and the tables. Despard had
been easygoing, omitting the touch of irony he always
put in his dealings with him. A. had admired his
handling of people; he was chummy and subtle at the
same time, he tried to say just enough without jarring
them and disturbing the cozy pleasures of Saturday
night, and he succeeded in this at times.

After midnight, when everything had closed, he had walked A. back to his house. They had not said good night there but had gone on pacing up and down the street. Despard had talked of his family. His father and grandfather had been printers, serious men bent on self-improvement; his grandfather had been on the barricades of 1848. "He's never elaborated on it," Despard said, "he was twenty-one at the time, and I think the rest of his life was an anticlimax, spent on little but *if*ing. We've had trouble with the police ever since, they have never forgotten. These two men are the reason I'm not such a puritan as the others. Two generations of teetotalers is enough to work up a thirst."

It was very cold in the room. A. put his head back under the blanket. It had been a pleasing evening, like evenings in his past when he was still a student about town and came home late from parties; there had been endless discussions in those days with no one ready to go to bed—but this had been better, it had been real, not about what they would do later, but about now. He had been aware of himself, walking there with a man like Despard. He looked around his room. His work clothes were lying on the floor, partly in a puddle of melted snow from his shoes; the brown paper shade from the window was torn, which he had not noticed before, and it was waving in the air blowing in through the cracks. His towel had fallen on the floor too, and was grey rather than white; he had forgotten to take his linen to the laundry woman.

What a repulsive mess, I'd like to stay in bed and not face it. Anne won't come because I wasn't here last night when I was supposed to be in. He decided it was nice that it was Sunday and no one would come and no one expected him. He clutched his feet and rolled himself up to keep as warm as possible. But a minute later he jumped out of bed, put on some clothes, lit the stove, and went out to get hot water.

He was going to do a room cleaning, but moving the bed uncovered so much dust that his courage failed him and he quickly pushed it back into place. He filled his basin, put it on the floor, and shivering scrubbed himself. He found a frayed but clean shirt which he put on, and his dark jacket. It had a small hole in front, and he pasted a piece of paper blackened with ink on the inside. The total effect, seen in the mirror, seemed acceptable; he ate a slice of bread and went to the party of Helen Peret.

He had felt his appearing there would cause her some consternation but he had underestimated her good manners; she hesitated only a moment as he stood in the doorway. Then she smiled and gave him her hand, and introduced him to half a dozen men and women, boys and girls really. The guests were sitting in a circle, and his entering created a silence until a young man began a story about a horseback-riding incident. Everyone listened, and a maid presented a tray with sherry and lemonade. A. took a glass and drank it down; he sat back and crossed his legs, discovered that he had lost the piece of paper behind the hole in his jacket, sat upright again with his glass in front of the hole, and finally looked at Helen. She caught his glance and gave him a wink which startled him. She was wearing a white dress, her hair was piled high on her head, and the impression of unapproachable brightness of the first time he saw her made sense again. He was asked no personal questions. These well-behaved people talked about generalities, and no one seemed to find anything unusual in his presence. How are they different from my old student friends, he asked himself, is it that they're all such *owners?* An hour went by in which he hardly spoke but drank many sherries in an increasing mood of irreality. Helen's mother came in to meet the guests; she nodded to A. and said, "Helen has told me about your exams. You must be very clever." A. looked modest. "You must come and have dinner one day soon, my husband loves talking about mathematics," her mother added. "I'd be delighted," A. mumbled and stared surprised at Helen. Now he felt a great warmth suddenly for all these people. He got up and went over to Helen. "You're terribly nice," he whispered to her, "You and your friends. I love you all."

"Come and I'll show you our conservatory," Helen said. She opened a door which he had thought lead into the garden, and they entered a greenhouse, a long glass-walled room filled with plants, ferns, crystal vases holding peacock feathers with their blind eyes, framed Chinese prints, curved little tables, a pile of copies of an Italian illustrated weekly, rattan chairs. It was warm and still in there, as in a pyramid tomb, he thought. "My father raises orchids," she told him. "Isn't it pretty here?" "Yes," he answered, thinking, what a frightening, desperate room, a chamber of horrors, all the ghosts of the nineteenth century in it.

XXXI

ALTHOUGH he was prone to staring into space, especially when he was supposed to study, he was not apt at or interested in self-analysis. If Anne or someone would have tried to prove to him that his real motives were not what he thought they were and that he was just an egoist in a more sublimated way than, for instance, his father, he would not have been shocked. He would have said that his motives made no difference to the world. He trusted himself. He had a long time ago come upon the words of a French revolutionary writer: "Our modern world practices cannibalism, in its civilized form," and that was indeed how he had begun to see it. It was obscene to be satisfied with such a world and unavoidable to react against it.

In the beginning, when he still discussed these things with others, his father had announced that "radicals" weren't moved by the physical miseries of the poor or the colored races, but by their own mental problems. He had not answered, but one thing seemed quite clear to him; physical anguish had to be translated into mental anguish before anything could ever be done about it, as the bodily pain of the sick had to be translated into the mental worry of the healer. It's possible to suffer from the idea of injustice as from a disease and it's a good disease, he had told himself. Without it, a man may starve, in silence. But I know enough mathematics to see that the idea that Babeuf or Marx or all of them together could *prove* socialism, as if it were another theorem of Pythagoras, is, regrettably, nonsense. The universe is not necessarily interested in human happiness.

It was his father's violent reaction which had made the Radical committee important. Joining them had brought with it a complete fall from the comfortable, normal, usual world to a cold room, cold water, hunger. And thus, in a mirrorlike way, it was as if it had at least knocked a chip off the paralyzing solidity of comfort, normalcy, and reality.

That it had done nothing of the sort became clear to him, paradoxically, through the disappearance— death, he assumed—of Wenster. Then it was obvious that he must go on, and join those whom Wenster himself had been the first to call, the others.

Can I do it, he wondered, do I have the hardness? This isn't half playing like the committee, it's leaving

not just your parents' home but all homes; opening a
door, even if you don't have to go through it, to
broken bodies in police ash cans, vanished men in
cells, gallows. Do I have the nerve to live with that
door opened? Think of *Michael Strogoff, the Czar's
Courier,* how brave he was; and then go all the way
beyond that to where with nothing behind you, you
are fighting your own world instead of its little con-
ventional enemies, you're fighting the Czar instead of
those poor slobs of Tartars, you're fighting king and
country instead of natives. He knew he could never
have done it rationally; you just had to make the
jump, and to hell with it all.

And it changed your ideas once more about women.

He wrote out on one of his cards: Wenster plus
Anne equals Despard plus Helen.

Without Helen I wouldn't have had the nerve yet,
she is my Mädchen aus der Fremde, unknowingly; she
is the girl you see once from a train window, you are
off to somewhere alone, the train has stopped in a
small town you do not know near the capital. Then, as
the train is gathering speed again, racing past streets
and houses in the early evening, a first lamplight here
and there, you see a young girl walking along a sidewalk going home, she stops in a doorway and turns
around for a moment, looking after the train. And all
longing, nostalgia, in you flows out toward her, an
almost unseen girl, and you would give your life for
her.

XXXII

THE DINNER invitation from her mother reached him at
the university. Idiotic, he thought, as if my old life is
catching up with me again, and who wants to have
dinner with the parents of the girl seen at dusk from
the speeding train? But it will be worth while finding
out if I'm still just a bit of a nice young man, or if I'll
be someone from another country; precisely in Mrs
Peret's dining room it should be pleasant to have
nothing behind you, to play a game like a criminal
with a stolen passport, like a revolutionary.

There were more guests than he had anticipated,
and he was seated near the end of the table, next to
the boy from the party who had discussed horses; they
seemed to be the only people invited by Helen. He
looked at her, at her mother and at her father, and
thought he indeed did not care about it all. He drank
his wine and did not talk.

Then he caught her glancing at him with concern,
pity almost. She thinks I'm tongue-tied.

I'll say something.

A gentleman held forth about the English aristocracy, a popular subject just then in the press, and
finished, "We could do with a class of that quality in
this country."

"The English aristocracy, sir," A. said, "will be remembered chiefly for articles of clothing and food, such as sandwiches, cardigans, and Wellington boots." He liked that and smiled at Helen, but she blushed.

I've embarrassed her, which serves her right. ". . . the Bank of England," the former speaker ended a sentence, looking severely at him.

There was a moment's silence and A. answered, "Well, you know Dante, E perchè l'usuriere altra via tiene."

A lady laughed nervously, and in the new general conversation he was ignored.

When coffee was served in a drawing room, Helen's father came over to him and asked, "What was that about usury?" Is this her father, he then wondered, she doesn't look like him; and he looks very much like another man here. Perhaps brothers? Shall I ask him who he is? "Dante wasn't talking about usury," he answered, "he put anyone in hell who makes money unnaturally, money from money, that is—all bankers."

"Oh," the man said and walked away.

A. left the room unnoticed, but as he waited for his coat, Helen came out into the corridor.

"I have to leave," he said to her. "I haven't said goodbye, I thought I'd better not—please tell your mother I wasn't feeling well."

The maid brought his coat. "Now I really won't pester you any more," he said to Helen.

"It's me," she answered, "I am the one who is sorry. Can you forgive me?"

"Well, yes," A. said, surprised. He opened the door.

"Don't be sad," she whispered hastily. "It'll be all right. I'll send you a message . . . perhaps I will love you too."

Outside he saw it was not even nine o'clock. There was a chance that Anne would be home. He'd go and see her. He descended the street. That day a thaw had set in and a yellowish fog hung between the houses; walls, trees, pavements, everything was soaking wet, the park lay in complete darkness, its gate closed, water dripping everywhere. Why was this girl, Helen, Helena, Hélène, so easily moved and why did she so tenaciously refuse to remain the girl seen in passing only? She was beautiful tonight, her bare arms. But she's a vestal virgin, impossible to imagine her taking off her slip and her panties and creeping into bed with somebody. But perhaps she would. But not for any man, for a cause—the cause of marriage preferably. Right now what appeals to her is not me but the cause of love-at-first-sight. I wasn't even lying, but it's love for her body, her physical being, not exactly for herself. She just lives in it and probably knows little about it.

XXXIII

SHE HAD told him she took piano lessons for which she went to the house of a French lady who had difficulty walking, and she now dropped these and instead spent that time in a tearoom nearby, where he joined her between his classes.

It was a place run by a women's association, full of wood curlicues, doilies and artificial flowers, and glass panels in the ceiling bathing it in a shadowless light like a secularized clerestory. There was never any other male customer but one very old gentleman with a dripping nose who had his daily tea there with his wife; when A. came in, the ladies turned their heads and followed him with their eyes to Helen's table. He always kept his overcoat on because of the old clothes he wore; he sat with his collar up, his legs stretched out, slumped in his chair. She leaned over the table toward him, her arms folded, and talked earnestly and with enthusiasm, like a social worker he thought: a little barrier of words against the problem of what they were actually there for. He told her about his father and his exile from home. She didn't argue against it as he would have thought nor implied that his poverty then was any less real. Since I'm not from South Hill, she may prefer my self-imposed attic.

"You are sure you're doing the right thing?" she once half asked however, "You do see your father's point of view?"

"Every action is Manichean," A. answered.

She said, "I'm afraid I don't know what that means," without showing much eagerness to find out.

He always left before her, just before her piano hour was up, and she always paid.

There was no longer any question of his coming to

her house, and when she talked about her parents and her friends, she made it sound like anecdotes from a different world he would neither want to nor be able to share. On two occasions he asked her to come to his room; once she did not answer, once she said, "What would your girl friends say to that?" But there was a specific kind of warmth in her; her face lit up when she saw him.

He had a vile cold one day; as he entered the warm tearoom, he felt his body turn clammy and thought he shouldn't have come. He sat down holding his handkerchief in front of his face. "I'll only stay a moment," he said, "I don't want you to catch my cold." In answer she got up and forced him to take off his coat; he was wearing his torn jacket and no tie. "To hell with those ladies," she said about the staring customers, a choice of words unusual and not quite suited to her. She lent him her own handkerchief and made him order a grog which, however, the tearoom served in an alcohol-free variety. After that she patted him on his hand and said, "You must take better care of yourself."

Often when she talked, he hardly listened but just studied her. He enumerated the wave of her hair, her cheekbones, her sea eyes, a noble face, but perhaps only the pale nothingness nobility of light things?, like the silver hair of an old crook senator, the white marble of our banks and palaces. Or the real beauty of coolness, of the ocean I have never seen.

The politics of beauty. Our morality and our hell

were born in the thoughts of parched men, sunstruck priests living on the fringes of an Africa which must have been so fearful to them, black, heathenish, fertile. And thus we have a hell that is hot, and evil that is dark.

Let us now proclaim a hell that is an ice field, and evil that is pale.

I want to find myself a gypsy to fall in love with, a dark dark girl, born from the earth and music. Abundant, not virginal.

XXXIV

HE WOULD look back upon those weeks as an interregnum of peace, and he imagined that he had known at the time it would not last and appreciated it especially and felt he deserved it because of that.

He did the work for his approaching university examination. It did not interest him just then, and he hated getting up early for morning classes. But the awareness of being a student still helped against cold, hunger, dirty clothes, and the long marches through inimical suburbs; he realized it was cheating somewhat to have such a source of comfort. Evenings he went canvassing and he usually signed up some men and women now.

He struggled through an hour or two each day of

working on the index, and that paid for the food, mostly bread and tomato paste, for light and coal; the rent had been paid up with the money from his mother. Anne came over at least Sundays, cooked as in the past, on the stove lid and on a spirit lamp, and stayed the night. She seemed a bit distracted and vague, but it was easier to get along with her, he thought, now that she had left off being so intense and enthusiastic. At rare moments did he find himself regretting this change and wanting back what was gone because it was gone. Then there were the after-noon sessions with Helen in the tearoom, the name of which was "The Sun." My confessional.

Only outwardly does it add up to a little routine; it's more than it seems, really, the best of it is hidden. There is more to my meetings with Helen than chastely sipping tea. To her, it must be like a prepara-tion at times, a trial period; after all, she is a reader of medieval romances. And those hours walking, knock-ing on doors, talking like an insurance salesman, aren't hours spent as an insurance salesman.

The country and the town were quiet, the papers filled with inanities. The president laid the first stone for a triumphal arch. One daily ran a contest for the most elegant way to peel an orange at a dinner. Public persons in the papers and illustrated magazines smiled winningly, or looked grave with the burdens of re-sponsibility. Just you wait, gentlemen.

Then things changed for him. The porter gave him

a note telling him to report to the office of the dean of the university, and there, after a long wait, he was received by a large man in a metallic blue suit. "I'm not the dean," the man told him, "the dean is busy, but I will convey to you his decision."

"Decision about what?"

"You have been suspended from this university, for one month. Your reinstatement will be contingent on a change in your behavior during that period."

"What's wrong with my behavior?" A. asked. And when he received no answer, "Are you talking about my behavior here at the school?"

"I can't speak for the dean," the man said, "but I'm confident he is not concerned with your private life."

"Well, how can I change my behavior when I don't know what you're talking about?" He suddenly thought of his examination. "I have an examination next week," he cried, "What about that? I would lose a whole year."

"You should have thought of that before. And I must ask you not to raise your voice in here."

"Before what?" A. asked. Oh go to hell you bastard, he thought. He got up to leave.

"One moment."

Have I misjudged them, will they let me do the exam? He turned around with a half-smile.

"I have a bill for you here," the man said. "You owe this school ten francs for the repainting of a door."

A. walked out without answering. He stood in the

street, in a light rain, and wondered where to go. Now I'm really free. I'll go see Despard. Not for advice; he'd say, leave us, finish your studies.

But the idea of talking about it with Despard made him feel better.

He became aware of a short, grey man who had been behind him for some time. I'm being followed, he thought, how about that. He turned a corner and waited. When he shows up, I'll grab him by his collar. He'll be sorry. That's just what I need right now.

But no one passed and when he finally looked around the wall of the house, the street was empty.

At the café across from the factory entrance, they told him that Despard had been fired and that they had not seen him all week.

XXXV

As HE got back to his room, wet and rather miserable, he found Anne sitting there, the stove lit, and his bed made. "What a marvelous surprise!" he cried. "Am I happy to see you!"

She smiled, stood up, but did not answer.

"It's been a foul day," A. said, "and no one to tell about it. I've been suspended from the university. But let me kiss you first." He held his face against hers. "God, I'm soaking wet. Wait . . ." He peeled off his coat and hung it over a chair, with some difficulty took off his shoes, and dried his face and hair on the towel. Anne had sat down again, and he put himself near the stove and shook the water out of his trouser legs. "You know, I'm supposed to do my candidate's exam next week," he said. "That would be a whole year gone to the devil."

She now looked concerned. "But that would be terrible," she answered. "It's because of your politics of course. . . . I think you should appeal. Even if you have to go and see your father. Have him go there for you! It must be possible to have them reconsider."

"Yes—" A. said. "They'd want at the least a promise from me about no more politics. Without that I'll never get back. The man I talked to looked as if he'd like to see me hanged. Sort of disconcerting: real hatred from someone you don't even know."

"Was it the chancellor?"

"I don't know—some big bald man."

He sat down beside her on the bed. "You should come back to us," Anne said, "that might be enough for them. And does it really make that much difference?"

"Perhaps not, perhaps you've been right from the beginning."

"Well—" she answered.

"You know, when you come to think of it, they're really incredible. Don't people have the damnedest, most incredible capacity for fooling themselves, for dividing up their minds into different compartments?

These men must have read Plato, and Herzen, and Robespierre; and they obviously don't say to themselves, 'it's all a fraud, but we're bowing to the government to keep our jobs'; that would at least be something, no, they've convinced themselves it's all proper and fine and there's no conflict between anything, and their heroes of the past were somehow different from the bums and radicals and reds of today."

Anne was pacing through the room without concentrating on his words. "How would you ever get back to your work?" she asked. "Look at you now; in a year you'll have forgotten everything you studied, and your clothes will be falling apart, but literally, and you'll sell your last books—"

"Oh, stop it," A. said, "I feel sorry enough for myself already. Let's eat."

She hesitated. "I had only come for a short visit," she said. "I hadn't planned to stay. I have to—"

"Oh, no, you can't leave me like this! I've got eggs, and bread, and there's even some beer. I'll fix it, you just sit there."

"No, no," she said, "that pot is filthy. Let me do it."

The room was not dark because the sky had cleared, it was freezing again and there was an almost full moon. The window was steamed over, in the morning that would be ice. As he came into her, she lay motionless, and then suddenly she began to move, to circle so frantically with her body that she almost threw him off. "Come," she whispered, and then she closed her eyes and lay still with her head sideways.

He bent over to kiss her and saw that she was crying.

"Anne," he asked, "what is it? Why are you upset?"

She shook her head, then she jumped out of bed. "Close your eyes," she said unexpectedly.

He could hear her get dressed. She sat on the edge of the bed, with her dress and coat on. She took his hand and told him, "You mustn't mind." "Mind what?" he asked. His heart started beating fast.

"I won't come back," she said. "I had come to say goodbye, but then you were so upset, and I couldn't . . . I shouldn't have, I shouldn't have made love with you— You must forgive me for that."

"I'll try," he answered with a laugh. She must have seen me with Helen, or heard about it, he thought, it's not serious. "Listen," he went on, "you know that's just nonsense. Of course you'll come back. What would this room do without you? Don't you suspend me too."

"I'm sorry."

"But why? Have you heard—" He was afraid to mention Helen in case she did not know after all. "Have they gossiped about me? I know I've been very vague. But I'm as faithful as an old dog. You're not jealous or something, are you?"

"Jealous?" She sounded surprised. "No, of course not. I'm never jealous."

"Then what is it all about?"

"There's someone else," she said. "Someone I'll live with, perhaps get married to . . ." Her voice trailed off.

"Someone you love?"

"Yes."

XXXVI

WHEN Anne had closed his door behind her, he lay still, stretched out on his back with his feet sticking out from under his blanket, staring at the ceiling and thinking in those precise words: I will now indulge in an orgy of self-pity.

But lying there, his effort to get tears in his eyes on account of Anne failed, and he found his head empty of any thoughts at all.

He dreamt that owls were flying through his room, owls with human faces; then he woke up again with a shock. Those were the harpies, he thought, plaguing that blind old king whatever his name was. They must have been symbols for bad memories, for memories of chances wasted, ignobilities, cruelties to others. The day you no longer feel you can undo what you did wrong and redeem yourself, you are old, and the day you no longer look forward but backward, you are blind. That's what that blind old man means.

But what did my dream mean, what is it warning me about?

I haven't hurt anyone. As far as Anne goes, she beat me to it, which serves me right of course.

I could free myself from this whole rotten mess, world, city, by creeping into my books. But who wants to be free by the grace and with the kind permission of some bloody government official in a blue suit; who wants to live protected by this murderous government? Damnation, even if Despard would quit now and ask for his job back, I'd still stick.

He thought he heard soft steps on the landing outside his door, and had several thoughts at the same moment, Anne come back, the police, Despard. He waited, poised to jump out of bed, ready to have a good cry with Anne; but he didn't hear another sound.

He saw his city as if from a great height, its silent streets bathed in the ever sharpening moonlight, the black shadows of the buildings drawing creneled edges on the bright pavement; and the city was empty, with no one breathing in it but himself, lying in his attic with his feet pointing west and his head east, and between him and nothing was only the miserably thin roof. He could almost look through it into the immovable sky, under which he was slowly wheeled eastward.

XXXVII

"But she wasn't invited," Helen was saying. "And my uncle and aunt would never have believed she would go anyway."

It had been a strange morning. He had got up and hastily poured out water to wash before remembering that the university was closed to him. He had crept back into bed then, but while he used to think he'd do about anything to be able to stay in bed mornings, it had lost its appeal and he got up again. He could have started on his daily quota of the Marco Polo index but he felt ill at ease in his room. He opened the window and a cold, dry wind jumped in and tore off the paper shade. The window fell shut; he propped it open. Sounds came in of women beating carpets, of the bell of a knife grinder pushing his cart through the street.

Outside, a low sky touched the roofs and the air seemed filled with an invisible dust of ice. He kept his eyes almost closed, and he was walking along a southern lake shore he had seen in a lithograph in one of the Marco Polo books or perhaps it was that stream where Michael Strogoff drowned or almost drowned. He drank a cup of coffee in a bar and went to the National Library. Eventually, they'd have his name on a list and some nasty or embarrassed clerk would point out that they couldn't allow him in either. He was going to get out the book he had planned to read for his examination, but then thought, to hell with it, and sat down where someone had left a stack of books on the table. He opened one and started reading. The hours crawled by; every time he was going to jump up he told himself, five more minutes, or, until that man turns his page.

Thus he had struggled through the morning, and when he finally left, he hurried to the tearoom, although he was an hour early. For the first time he arrived there before Helen.

When Helen came in, her first words were, "Guess what happened!"

Thank God, something nice, he said to himself, but it was a story about a party, he only half listened. What idle nonsense, he thought. Should I tell her what happened with me at the university? She wouldn't react the right way. He felt annoyed at what he imagined her answer would be. And he felt a pain of longing for Anne—how could he have been bored by her intensities, by the eagerness with which she read and discussed pamphlets, carried newspaper clippings around, wrote letters to people she didn't know?

"You're not listening," Helen said.

"Yes, I am. No, as a matter of fact, I'm not. Does it matter?"

"No," she said, smiling.

She looked very pretty and that made it worse. "I'm glad you realize it yourself," A. said, "Why then do you waste your time on these banalities? Why do we talk about them? Why think about them? Don't you have anything else on your mind? Who are these people so absorbed in their own damn pleasures? They're welcome to it, I don't care, but why give it a second thought? Who in Jesus' holy name cares if your uncle breaks his tooth on the buckshot in his Christmas goose or your cousin quarrels with her fiancé or for that matter, breaks her neck? Or who—"

He stopped himself. Helen had turned red. For the first time since he knew her, she looked, not offended as he had expected, but piteous. He got up, almost knocking over his chair, and fled from the tearoom.

XXXVIII

HE VISITED his old student cafés that evening, skipping only the Crystal Café where he could not go back after the tale he had told the owner the last time. He was going "to stir things up," he had decided.

The first moments were the hardest. It was easier to face the ire of a policeman than the contempt of a headwaiter or owner of a bar; you get a welcome as a customer to which you have no right because you are not going to be just a customer; you sail in under a false flag. But it was not unheard-of in those cafés for a student to get up and address a room, mainly filled with students too, about some student business.

He began in a place which was crowded and smoky and where no one paid attention to his entrance. He went straight to the counter where the barman was setting up steins of beer at great speed, and picked one up as an alibi. He was frozen and hungry and a big moist jug of beer was actually the last thing in the world he wanted. He backed against a wall. God, I hate this, he said to himself, they'll think I'm an exhibitionist, no one would believe how much I hate it. He cleared his throat and said, "Fellow students!"

A comparative quiet followed those words as everyone looked to see who was speaking. It did not last and A. continued against an increasing volume of voices, "I have been suspended from the university."

He caught the eye of the headwaiter whose expression changed in that instant from indulgence to total disgust. So striking was the change that it broke A.'s trend of thought. He doesn't look disgusted because he is a conservative, he thought, or indeed for any political reason; he doesn't know nor care what this is all about. He simply now smells in my presence here something averse to the selling of beer, to the Spirit of Commerce. He's disgusted at what he considers my stupidity, partly. It makes me a member of an alien tribe to him, a nomad among farmers, a salamander in a goldfish pond, an anomaly and a threat. There's the very heart of the matter, he doesn't have to reason about it, it's in his blood. That headwaiter's contempt is the lifeblood of our society.

He repeated lamely, "Fellow students!" Someone clapped and there was laughter. A. laughed too. "I've been suspended for political reasons, for socialist propaganda I guess they call it in their files, though no one has come out and admitted any reason to me."

It was quieter now.

"I'm not asking for your sympathy or help," A. said. "I knew the risks like everyone. But there are some principles involved, general principles."

At a table opposite him, a dispute arose but was hushed by others.

"There's the principle of the autonomy of the university; for a long time now we have maintained that outside authority has no right to interfere with us at all."

He got considerable approval on this point; the headwaiter, who had put down a tray and made his way toward him, was stopped and involved in an argument about letting him speak.

"But," A. said, "that's not my main point. My point is political."

"We'll hear you on autonomy but not on politics," someone shouted and was applauded.

"The autonomy of the university is marvelous," A. said, "but it's a relic, a tradition. It is time to make some new forms. We, the intellectuals, if you permit the word, should stop being a cozy little group and should maybe try to do some thinking for everyone in this city. This city needs a conscience." There was so much talking now that he had trouble being heard. It helped him too, though; he lost his inhibition about raising his voice. A student pulled at his sleeve to get his attention and made A. spill half his beer down his coat. "This university was on the side of science once against the Inquisition," he said. "The truth about the sun and the moon and the earth was more important than the fear of shaking up snug ideas. Don't be afraid of heresy. Don't be afraid of twentieth century heresy, the socialist critique of the world, which is—" He stopped, for booing now drowned out his voice. There were some shouts of approval too, he thought. He pulled several pamphlets out of his pocket and thrust them in the hands of those near him; some accepted them, some dropped them on the floor. He saw the headwaiter and the barman both making for him, he turned around and walked out.

In the street he realized he had not paid for his beer, which pleased him immensely.

The next café he entered was almost empty, and he knew he would not work up the nerve to speak there. He pretended to look for a friend, leaving pamphlets on the tables on his way out.

Then came a place where it was really a success, he felt. They let him finish there, and a student got up, someone he knew by face as a prominent member of a fraternity and various sports clubs, and took up the same theme, ending startlingly with the words, "When the workingmen of this town go on strike, so must we."

A. pushed his way over to him in the tumult following that statement and asked, "How did you know about the strike? What is your name?" Before the man could answer, a waitress started tugging at A. "That's a detective who just came in," she said in a low, hoarse voice. A. looked around and she directed him toward the kitchen door with a nod.

In the kitchen an old man was sweeping the floor and ignored him as he first opened a closet, then found the back door. Outside, A. waited in a doorway across the street, expecting the student who had talked about striking to come out too, but no one appeared. After a while he went home.

XXXIX

In a street in the eastern outskirts of the town, adjacent to the glassworks, he was beaten up. That was known to be a tricky area and they did not visit it alone; A. went with an old man, a retired glassblower with a grinding cough who had once lived there. A. was sent to meet this man in a workers' restaurant, where he found him reading a book at an empty table;

a thin, grey man with iron spectacles. They shook hands without a word but when A. led the way to the omnibus stop, the glassblower looked at him in surprise and muttered, "I'm not sick, we can go on foot."

They set out silently. The sun had vanished behind the houses, the light had become undirected and shadowless and was everywhere, cold and glaucous, filling the sky. Under this sky A.'s companion looked very old. "Since they know you there, I guess you should do most of the talking," A. said to him, thinking that would please the man.

They came finally to the first block of workers' houses built by the glassworks. They were two-story structures, with front and back entrances to the units they were split up into, made of dark grey wood and asphalt blocks. "God, they look miserable," A. said, more to himself. The old man coughed, cleared his throat, and remarked, "These are not the glassblowers. These are where the glassboys live." They knocked on a door, and a child let them into a room where an old couple sat at a table. "That's a glassboy," the old man said, pointing to the man at the table who was not much younger than he himself. "He's night shift." The couple nodded at them, and offered them glasses of tea, almost colorless. White tea like Chinese coolies; what does a glassboy do, A. wondered, looking at the trembling hands of the man they were visiting. They talked. The man said, yes, he had heard of the International, those people had once tried to make a union but not for his line of work; he'd be ready to sign up but he had no money; "We're just a bit difficult this month," his wife said. The glassblower seemed undecided, and A. took it upon himself to say, "You can owe us your dues until it's convenient."

They tried four more families in the house (at two doors there was no answer), and as they came out again into the twilight, the glassblower said thoughtfully, "Now, I'm not sure you were right before . . . if a man pays for the movement, he knows it's his, he feels he owes it something. That sounds upside down to you, but the fact is . . ." "Let's go in here," A. said, turning him toward a door, for in the half-light he saw some men emerge and slowly walk toward them in an odd way. He knocked on the door, but before it opened, one of the men came up to them and hit A. against the side of his head. The door opened and closed again. A. turned, holding his hands in front of his face; he was hit again, and he felt a tooth break. He tried to hit back, and beside him he heard the glassblower wheeze and cough. "Leave him alone," he shouted, and then his legs gave out from under him.

As he opened his eyes, he was half leaning against the wall. He took a deep breath. The old man was sitting beside him, laughing softly. "Are you all right?" A. asked, "are you all right?"

"They never touched me," the glassblower answered, still chuckling.

"I'm glad you're amused," A. said. He pulled out his

handkerchief and wiped his face. It was full of blood, and he felt his face swell.

"They were glassboys too," the glassblower stated. "The owner pays them to break up organizing. They've done that for years. But they don't scare me. Let's go on."

"Well, sure, why not," A. answered, "there's nothing like a friendly little tussle." This sarcasm was lost on the old man who stood up and knocked again on the door which had opened and closed before.

They worked the entire street to where it ended in a field. In one house they gave A. witch hazel, and he dipped his handkerchief in it and kept dabbing his face which seemed to swell more and more. Night had fallen, and every time they came out of a house, A. expected to see men waiting for them again, but the street remained empty. The wind had risen, and it was bitter cold now.

Then he and the old man began walking back toward town. Once there were quick steps behind them and A. jumped aside, but it was only a boy clutching bottles, running an errand.

There were hardly any street lamps in this part of town. Here and there in a window an oil lamp flickered, or a miserable candle; it was very dark. Behind these walls, so many horrors; tears carrying away with them not only the hopes of young men, but the hopes of old men too; even life itself. He felt tears well up in his own eyes, he did not know from pain or from pity, and he said to the glassblower who was now walking a step ahead of him, "You could at least ask if it hurts, damn you." The old man walked on even faster but did not answer.

XL

HIS CAFÉ SPEECHES brought him the visit from a university friend, someone from the earliest days, from before the Radical committee even. It was a shock to A., a pleasant one, to see this man suddenly appear in the doorway. You do need your friends. He pushed dirty clothes under the bed, said, "Please sit here, that was very nice of you to come," and ran downstairs for beers.

"We talked about you," the man told him, "after your speech in that bar—" He looked at A. "Were you beaten up?"

"No. I fell. What did they think of the speech?"

"Oh, you know, they're not a very serious bunch. But they, all of us, are mad that you were suspended. You were one of the most serious among the lot."

"But you think I'm crazy."

"Aren't you?"

A. laughed. "I miss my friends," he said.

"Don't you need them?"

"Yes."

"Then why are you avoiding us?"

"I'm broke—my father cut me off."

"You know that doesn't faze us. That man who had spent all his money on the girl from—"

"It's not the same," A. interrupted him. "I know about that kind of solidarity. I'm doing this on purpose. I've cut myself off, really."

"Well, I've come here to lure you back," the friend told him.

There was a silence. "Drink your beer," A. answered.

"I understand a revolutionary workman," the other finally said, "or a coolie, they're at the bottom, we're on top, they want to turn the world around. Nothing complicated about that. But you, even with holes in your jacket you're not a workman. Why attack your own class?"

"Oh God," A. said, "now I know again why I stopped going to the fraternity house. I hate that kind of talk. Are we all to be animals then, and kick and squeeze out what's not our kind? You mean there's no right and wrong, only satisfying your goddamn own self? I know if you'd give a socialist workman a nice bank account, he'd calm down quickly enough. That's precisely it, our morality is the product of our income." He waved his hand to stop the other man from interrupting. "I know that's nothing new, but it was still an amazing discovery . . . and aren't we pathetic when we try to prove how right and righteous it is, our view of the world and our fellow men, and of the white race, and the whole setup, how natural, how responsible, how historic, how everything? It's just instinct, my friend, yes, it's just *smell*. You know how when you take a newborn rat and put cat smell on it, a mother cat will let it suck with her kittens? Well, our moralities and solidarities are as blind as that, just instinct smell-love, they're just the smell of money, the sweet smell of property."

"Then tell me this—watch it, now—if that's true for me and all my horrible cohorts, why isn't it true for your ideas too? Why are they more valid? Is that theory about one's money shaping one's ideas just a wagon you climb on and off as you please?"

"It's less true for us," A. said, "because once your eyes are opened to this universal fraud, once you've seen it, if only for a minute, you've freed yourself from it—at least up to a point."

"Like a Buddhist frees himself from the rebirth cycle by goodness?" the friend asked ironically.

"Yes, precisely!" A. cried.

"And so you're not coming back to us?"

"No. I think not. I hope not," A. said.

XLI

A MEMORY or a half-dream of a visit to a city in another country, in early summer, a ride along freshly washed streets to a park with a palace in it, the trees in heavy green foliage, birds singing, bushes with bunched small white flowers, jasmine, light paths of pebbles. It was either a visualized story or a real visit as a small child with his father; I should ask him one day, he thought. It had surely been morning, the wide flagstone steps of the stairs had been radiant in the morning sun. He had been allowed inside, a sight-seeing tour or a dreamt audience with a Hapsburg king, he did not know; there were very wide, rectangular windows in the rooms, opened halfway down, with yellow draperies from ceiling to floor, and all the sounds and perfume of summer blowing in. An old man was sitting in one of these bright rooms. "This is the beauty of life as it can be," the man said, "counterbalancing dreariness and ugliness, this must be conserved, it is the conservative dream. But I will say this to you, if you have not participated, you cannot understand."

But he could easily understand. Standing at one of those windows and looking out over the grass touched by the wind, it was simple enough to understand that it seemed inconceivable, the will to destroy this, the only human setting as pure as a forest or a pasture, that there was a fine happiness in it, also a discipline which made it deserved almost, the discipline of aesthetics, of silk dresses, starched collars, chamber music, understated emotions. The people in such rooms had begun a new race, different from other men as men are different from dogs and cats, freed from the vulgar mechanics of life.

But not by defeating these mechanics; on the contrary, by delegating them to others.

He understood that summer morning and could be nostalgic for it as if it had been part of his own youth.

XLII

THERE WAS a break in the weather, what his mother would have called false spring; during the afternoon the iron-colored sky broke, high cloud banks came towering in from the west with gaps of blue between them, and a soft wind ran through the city. He realized he had stopped shivering, sitting in his overcoat in his room where the stove had gone out, and as he opened the window he heard the sounds from the street carried without their winter dullness. He took his remaining money out from under the book on the mantelpiece; as he hastily put on his shoes, his coat swept half the index cards onto the floor but he was in too much of a hurry for the street to pick them up. He marched to the corner of his block in a vague dread that someone could be coming to see him just then and that he would have to go back upstairs, and he only calmed down on the avenue which led into the heart of the city. I'm in a slight frenzy, he said to himself, perhaps it's because of Anne's desertion. Frustration. It's disgusting the way I'm living, like a high school boy poisoning yourself with dreams. Or like travelers in the desert or in little ships for months without women, everything around them must become obsessive, it makes daily things hard and inimical, it metallizes the world. Unless they like men better than women anyway, of course. Feminineness is softening, like vines covering a sharp, unpleasant to the touch iron gate.

It was getting dark, but here in the center of the town lights went on everywhere, shop windows shone in gaslight and electric lamps, and the sidewalks were still crowded with people awakened from their hibernation. He counted his money with one hand without taking it out of his pocket, and thought it would be nice to spend it all that day. He entered a restaurant, but as he looked at its menu it seemed a terrible waste to use money for feeding yourself alone at a table when bread and cheese would do as well, and he left again. He was drawn on toward the poor streets—a very different kind of poverty from the dry, cold poverty of the industrial suburbs; this was moist, warm; instead of misery, sin. Well, sin—here the poor played the game instead of remaining outsiders; they were the house serfs, so to speak. He came to a corner bar called the Stella, from where a little sidestreet led to an army barracks. That street had no name sign, but it was known by everyone as Stella Street, and here girls, of the cheapest category, were to be found. He walked down to the gate where a sentry stood, a red-faced recruit slumped over his rifle who looked

not more than fifteen. "Nice evening," A. said; the
soldier straightened himself up and looked angrily at
him. It must be too early; no girls were on the sidewalks. He entered a little bar which had an artificial
plant in the window, painted a spotty red. Two girls
were sitting at the counter, one very young and thin,
one much older and rather fat. They looked at him
without enthusiasm and continued their conversation.
He sat down and stared at the bottles, and at his black
eye in the scratched mirror. Even Despard wouldn't
approve of this, none of them would, and they are
right of course, about prostitution being corruption,
not these poor creatures but those men who pocket
half or God knows how much of the money, corruption of the city itself; but still the idea of a woman
selling the use of her body, a woman you have never
seen before undressing herself naked for you at a
price, is breathtaking. A barmaid appeared from behind a curtain, wiping her mouth and still chewing,
and he ordered a gin.

The heavy girl took her pocketbook and left, and he
could see her starting to walk up and down outside.
He looked at the young, thin one; she looked back
with the beginning of a little professional smile and he
turned his eyes away. I can't, he told himself, it's too
risky that she's sick, and she is too young for me to
ask her to do something different, she'd be contemp-
tuous and I'd feel bound to try and impress her with
my manliness as if she'd give a damn. The other one,

with her it doesn't matter. He paid for his gin, smiled apologetically at the thin girl who ignored him, and went out into the street. The heavy woman walked on as he asked her how much it cost, not taking him too seriously as a potential client, "Ten francs," she said. He agreed, it was less than he had expected and left him some money. It was two houses away, he climbed after her up the staircase and stood in a little dark room. She waited and said, "Well?" and he hastily counted out her money.

"Lie down," she said.

Right at the end she stopped a moment and looked at his face, as if curious, and he loved her for that. Back out in the street, he said warmly, "Good night, thank you." She seemed surprised and nodded.

He walked into the Stella Bar and bought another gin. Now I'm free again to go back to the strike, he said to himself, tomorrow. I will send a note to Helen apologizing for the tearoom scene.

It's pleasing, coming from a woman and thinking about another, a poor man's Stendhal scene, a being in touch with the world.

XLIII

A BASEMENT ROOM in the old riverport area had become their meeting place, since the day they were fired from their jobs and no longer had to go to factories at the edge of town; some men even slept in it. It was the guards' room of a warehouse which stood empty and where no one ever set foot.

The weather was still too warm for February. Incessant rains descended on the town, and although the guards' room was not cold, it was miserably damp with a steady drip of water from the ceiling beams and pipes onto their heads. Here, at a table covered with a blanket to provide a smoother surface, A. was copying a statement, for multiplication on the gelatine hectograph someone had brought.

The statement was the product of days of debate and shouting. Their organization did not exist on paper in the world of officials, and thus could not negotiate; therefore it was signed by a Strike Committee of ten, some members of the International Association, and others not. They said they were airing long-unremedied grievances. (The original plan of a mass meeting of factory workers had been given up when it became clear it would have been suicidal for their group).

One of the printers working for them had withdrawn, and the other had his workshop sealed by the police, and thus their documents were now produced and multiplied in the same way A. had once put out a class newspaper in high school. "It will be said," he copied the end of the text on the sheet, "that we are making war on society. However, it is the present peace which is really war, war on the lowly." Nice, he said to himself. The actual demands of the statement were both vague and far-reaching, and even suggested sharing management and profits of some of the biggest and worst factories—"the profits created by our hands." Since there wasn't a chance that demands of theirs, any demands, would be met, they had decided asking so much instead of just the traditional shorter hours or better wages, and security. They wanted to be heard, and be counted—by their colleagues rather than by the owners or the government. That, they had agreed, could only come about by demonstrations. Finally, the statement asked for abolition of the system whereby a person drafted into the army could pay for a replacement, "the poor man's army."

"What about force?" someone asked Despard. "Force, violence, I mean. If we strike and they bring in strike breakers, do we try to stop them? If a foreman hits me, do I hit back?"

"Not if he's bigger than you."

"We can't be pacifists abroad and fight at home."

Despard answered, "In the end, we've agreed on that, it's all a matter of force, whether tested or not. My idea is that we must be Machiavellian, that we have every right to be Machiavellian. That is to say, resist force with force if we have a chance and not resist it if it's hopeless. But that's my private policy. I'm a different kind of pacifist. I think civil war may be a legitimate war."

A. had put the statement on the hectograph and was pulling off copies. The large sheets, with big letters in purple ink, some not too legible, were passed around.

"Do we really believe in this? Do we really believe revolution is made like this?"

"The French revolution of 1848 was started by *Le National,* one tiny newspaper."

"Printed on a hectograph?"

"No, but the *National* ran off less than three thousand copies in February 1848."

"How do you know?"

"I know. It's history."

A. was trying to get the purple stains off his hands in a basin of water with pumice stone when they called him. Water from the ceiling had dripped onto the gelatine sheet and washed out several words. The whole thing had to be done again. He shook his hands dry. The water is dripping in my sleeves, and I'm tired. Worst of all, I'm bored. This can't be what it's like, either—to be a revolutionary.

XLIV

HE HAD written to Helen and explained his outburst in the tearoom as caused by his trouble with the university. She wrote him back and he thought he detected a note of disappointment almost at this reason; "But you were right," she wrote, "our lives and conversations are inane. I want to change." And she went on to say that she would come again to see him at their old place.

That answer did not make him particularly happy. He would have preferred her to be proud and furious, and wronged. I'll exaggerate, he thought, and he wrote to her to come to his room instead. He took that note to her house, and then went back home and started on a frenzied cleaning. Halfway through he thought the room had been better before, romantic instead of just crummy; but he had gone too far to stop. His room had had the kind of dirtiness which, untouched, he could live in, but now that it was stirred up, it repelled him and he had to finish. It was another hour's work, and when he had washed off the smell of soot and household soap, he heard the church clock strike ten and cursed, for now she would surely not come any more that evening.

The following morning he was sitting sleepily at his table shuffling his index cards, when there was a knock on the door and she walked in. He jumped up.

"Good morning," she said. She began a smile, then stopped. "You don't look pleased. Am I interrupting you in your work?" she asked.

"Oh no, I am very happy you came," he said. He thought, damn, why didn't she come last night when there was a candle in the window and I was shaven. "Please sit down," he asked, turning the chair around to make her face away from the unmade bed.

"Can I take off my coat?"

He took her fur coat and hung it on a nail in the door.

"You were having breakfast," she said.

He took the piece of bread and cheese from the table and threw them in the paper basket. When she's gone I'll fish them out again. They do look repulsive.

He sat down opposite her. "It's too cold for you in here," he said, "we should go to a café and have some coffee."

Helen looked at him and began to laugh.

He laughed too. Here I've worked so hard at getting her here, but her presence is really disturbing more than anything else; she makes me feel slovenly. Even just touching her seems preposterous now. I sound like a little housewife, why does she instill me with this cleanliness mania?

"Don't you have—doesn't someone, your mother or someone, help you with your room?" she asked, looking around.

"My mother always wants to come, but I've stopped her so far. She'd be upset. She's actually sick in bed right now, we have a big lunch together once a week and she canceled yesterday because—you're not comfortable, are you?"

"I am a bit chilly," she said. "Perhaps I'll put my coat back on."

He brought back her coat, she wrapped herself in it, and smiled at him. "Tell me about the university," she said, "and about the strike committee and everything."

"I'm not free to tell you 'everything,' " he answered. Imagine all those layers, first fur, then that lovely heavy wool from some English island, then silk, more silk probably, and then her skin, very soft and shiny and virginal. I always thought this religion of virginity was barbaric, a subtle way to subjugate women, with all the miseries it causes, the pagan blood sacrifice of the wedding night—but perhaps it does have its meaning, a man-made beauty joined on to nature. The myth of virginity does make her seem different. It would be lovely to see her, just see her, naked.

He told her about the basement room without saying where it was, and the hectograph under the dripping water. It sounded better now, almost as romantic as she imagined it to be, and he felt in a hurry suddenly to go back there. She liked him for that and as she said goodbye, she asked if she could come again.

XLV

FOR ALMOST every factory and workshop, men were found willing to smuggle in the statements and distribute them. That part of the plan went off without a hitch, though they realized there were bound to be

workmen who would take their pamphlets to the foreman or the manager. The committee split into groups
and called on the factory administrations and on the
ministry "to discuss their demands." In no place but
the ministry were they even let in, and there a porter
told them after an hour's wait that all the gentlemen
of the department were too occupied to see them. This
was expected; unexpected was the quiet, the absence
of policemen or threats. We're being given enough
rope to hang ourselves, they said.

Leaflets were ready calling for a strike in the town
to start in a day, and during one frantic night these
were distributed in all the workers' quarters. Stay
home, let the machines work by themselves, it said.
When the last street had been covered, it was getting
light, and they closed out the basement room and
moved their things to the backroom of a café in the
stockyards district. Two men who had nowhere to go,
wanted to go on sleeping in the basement, but the
committee decided that was too dangerous and instead held a collection for boardinghouse money for
them.

They were to get some sleep, but few did. Haggard
and unshaven, they prowled around to see how the
strike call would be received. It was hard to judge;
people were too suspicious to show any reaction in
public. In some parts of the town, members of the
International Association had loosely organized themselves and chosen a spokesman, and these showed up

at the new office in the stockyards and delivered optimistic reports.

The following morning the committee members posted themselves at various strategic points. A. stayed with Despard's group of four, although no one had asked him to—except for Despard they had been more or less ignoring him of late. They met at the café across from the iron foundry. It was closed, and they huddled in the doorway. There was no one to be seen but a few men at the factory gate who did not look like workers; they were policemen in civilian clothes.

The first whistle blew to announce the day shift, and figures started looming up everywhere: within a minute the empty avenue was filled with people. It was as if they had all waited for each other, as if no one wanted to be first, and no one wanted to stay behind.

There was never much inclination among these men to converse at this early hour, but now it was unnaturally still. Only the shuffle of feet was heard as they entered the factory gate.

"Goddammit," Despard said. "Dammit to hell. It's a failure."

"The bastards, the dirty bastards."

"They're just afraid," A. said.

"Oh, what do you know about it," one of the group snarled at him. "You're just a damn student. I never knew what you want with us anyway."

"It so happens I no longer am a student—" A. began bitterly.

Despard interrupted him. "It so happens," he said sharply, "that my student friend here was thrown out of school for us. I don't want to hear a word against him, unless you want a good solid kick in the ass. Now let's go home. There's nothing for us to do here."

XLVI

WHEN A. was standing in front of his building, he thought, this sudden ending of all that work is really too much of an anticlimax to cope with, the idea of climbing up those stairs and working on the index of that damn Italian in China is nauseating.

Almost unthinkingly he clung to the company of Despard, whom he expected to be in the café backroom, and that was where he went. It was a long way back to the stockyards, and he avoided the main streets—I don't want to look in the faces of those smug bastards with their hot breakfasts in their bellies. Despard was in the office alone, and as he saw A. come in, he cried, "You're the first one! Welcome."

A. let himself down in a ramshackle chair and looked at him with surprise.

"Do you know?" Despard asked.

"Know what?"

"The ironworkers walked out. An hour after morning shift."

"No!"

"The lot. Maybe ten or twenty stayed behind at first. But the machines had to be stopped. So they left too." And Despard suddenly jumped up, pulled A. to his feet, and embraced him.

In the late afternoon, they went to reconnoiter. The foundry was lying dark, the gates closed. Nothing stirred in the half-light; the wind blew across the empty courtyard.

The next day an article appeared in *The People*, carried with minor variations in the other papers. The National Foundry was closed to enable a screening of the work force by its administration. Foreign agitators, and treasonous, self-seeking local elements had created disorder among the employees. Thus at a vital juncture in the development of the country, a blow had been struck at the national industry and the welfare of every single citizen. Of course the government would know how to deal with this, but no one could blame the citizens of the town for already showing their just wrath. Reservists of the officer corps and other supporters of the law were meeting to see to the protection of property and if necessary to the chastisement of the saboteurs.

Four hours later the committee was on the street with an "Open letter to the people of the capital" answering the attack; a very sober paper, its main item was a list of profits of the foundry and a list of wages of its men.

There were several dozen volunteers to take this

letter all over town. A. was posted at one end of the Quay Bridge; on the other sidewalk stood another volunteer, a young man from Despard's designing room. They had never talked much to each other, but the young man had made a point of greeting A., which not all of them did. He was called Caleb and his presence across the street helped.

The sky had cleared, and it was freezing again; a harsh blistering wind blew across the river, and the first office workers and housewives to appear hurried along, huddled in coats and scarfs. But a brightness in the light and its reflections on the little waves showed, A. thought, that in not so many weeks this endless winter was coming to its end.

A. and Caleb nodded at each other. "Here we go," A. shouted. They opened their parcels of leaflets wrapped in newspaper, and started handing them out to the passers-by.

Every once in a while, someone would accept one, glance at it and stuff it in his pocket. Others just refused to take them, shaking their heads without looking at A. But most people accepted the paper in what was mainly a reflex, and after a glance let go of it in a dead movement, with repulsion, as if their hand muscles were suddenly paralyzed and could no longer exert pressure. We've worked so hard on those handwritten purple ink sentences and here the beggars don't even read them.

The hard wind got hold of those abandoned leaflets,

and they rose and fluttered above the bridge, like a little stylized flock of birds, a flight of paper swallows in an Oriental opera. They hovered in the air and came down again on the still muddy pavement, where they were chased and picked up by A. and by the other man across the street from him. Some landed on the river and floated away. Some seemed to go on rising until they had dissolved in the cold blue sky above the town.

XLVII

WHEN HE turned the corner of the stockyard, he saw several men enter the café, and everything about them, their dark coats, their bearing, made clear that they were not customers of the place, and foreign to these littered streets, torn fences, smells of congealed blood and frozen dung. He bent over to tie his shoe, made a half turn and walked left instead of right without further looking, before the conscious thought that these were policemen had even registered. That pleased him; I'm learning to be a professional, he thought.

The street ended at a marshalling yard, he turned left again and started the road back to the center of town. There was nowhere to go now really.

My room—if they're at all serious about this,

there'll be someone there waiting for me. He still had some pamphlets, which he threw away; then he went to the public library, and sat in a corner reading Alexandre Dumas, and when they closed at six, he went to Anne's house. An old lady opened the door and told him she no longer lived there. He was too tired to do any more walking, and with his last money he took the omnibus to the professor from the Radical committee.

The professor said he was happy to see him, but acted very nervous. The news was all over town; the police had arrested everyone connected with the strike they had been able to lay their hands on. The iron foundry had been "militarized" and notices were posted saying that by twelve noon of the next day all strikers would be deserters.

"I'm frightfully sorry I can't put you up here," the professor said. "It's not myself I'm afraid for, you do understand that. I can't hazard the survival of the committee by being involved—"

"Yes of course," A. said, "I understand."

Back out in the street; a dark windy evening. The bastard could at least have fed me something. Surely he didn't anticipate the police breaking in at dinner time and interrogating his guests. Oh well, he's probably right, perhaps they're following me. He liked the image of policemen dashing into the dining room; he was so cold and hungry that he would have gone on eating his soup, nothing could have stopped me from that. Eating your soup hidden in a cupboard, run through by a sword. The death of Wallenstein, in some old lithograph. He was lightheaded and thought it was really quite funny. In a shop mirror he straightened his clothes, combed his hair with his fingers, and then he set out for his father's house.

The maid at least seemed glad to see him. "Your mother is not well," she said. The upstairs bedroom door opened and closed, and his father appeared at the landing.

They looked at each other.

"I'm glad you have finally seen the error of your ways," his father said. "Let us hope it was not too late. Your poor mother is very weak."

XLVIII

HE WAS sitting in his room amidst his old pictures, his school books, a bed made by someone else, tight and straight as only women are able to do it; eating cold meat from a plate taken from the kitchen, for he had not felt up to telling his father that he was hungry and hadn't had any dinner.

The light had been blessedly low in the bedroom and his mother had not noticed how bedraggled he was. She did not seem changed; her face was flushed but her voice sounded strong and she was not any thinner. They did not know or would not say what exactly was the matter with her. "It's just the winter that got me down," she declared. For the first time in his life he visualized the possibility that she, in fact that anyone closely connected with him, would die. That moment marks the end of your youth, he thought.

She did not know about the manifesto and the strike, and if his father had read about it in the paper, he would not associate such outlandish and almost apocalyptic goings-on with his cold and dirty-looking student son. When they emerged from his mother's room, his father had given him a short handshake, embarrassed, shy, perhaps guilty?, and muttering something about paperwork in the study, had vanished down the stairs.

A., indulging in the comforts of a world which, he sternly told himself, he never wanted to be his again, went to the laundry room in the attic, where he took off every thread of clothing he wore, rolled it all into a ball and put it in a laundry closet. His old shoes he shoved behind a suitcase. He looked around the door to make sure there was no one about, and then went naked down the steps and to the bathroom where a tub had been filled for him. He was so dirty that he liked the idea of such a total break. After that, he sat at the window in his room, his arms sticking halfway out of the sleeves of his high school bathrobe.

What a strange man, this father, he thought, a stranger, I hadn't seen him for a year and would perhaps not have recognized him in the street. It seemed actually decent now of this man to bother so, to express happiness that A. had abandoned his wild ideas, as he assumed—A. had not answered yes or no—; that he even felt the need to hold forth about president and country. For why should he bother really, why should he feed me and house me? If I hardly recognize him, he hardly recognizes me, I am sure. He engendered me. But that's a blind proceeding. He is doing his duty, he would indeed be dumfounded if it were suggested that it was not his duty. Only the demands of an even higher duty could compel him to throw me out. His life is framed within that rigid structure, man-made, a little time- and place-given set of rules and taboos, which to him, however, is the universe, eternal and self-evident.

Then why should I feel guilty for playing his game, for letting him keep me alive under false pretenses? It is a game like any other, you join it or you don't. I'm humoring his false presumptions since they're not false to him, they give sense to his existence.

XLIX

FOR ONE WEEK A. lived what he called "this scrubbed life"; nothing like a bath in the morning and a stomach full of hot porridge to blur your sense of justice. His father gave him five hundred francs, "your monthly allowance and to catch up and pay your debts." A. earmarked the money for the International Association and accepted with such obvious gratitude that for the first time since his return, the man smiled at him.

He had a contact address for emergencies and there he learned that many had gone into hiding; no one knew if Despard was still free. They needed money desperately for the fugitives from the police, and A. kept only ten francs from the five hundred for himself. The foundry had reopened; there were soldiers all over the place. A. remembered the exasperation with which he had read the diaries of those Russian revolutionaries who always went to their old rooms for just one more visit and were promptly arrested, and he was not going to make their mistake. He wrote a note to the Marco Polo author, announcing that he had had to leave the city because of a death in the family, and that the manuscript could be picked up in his room. Then he no longer thought about anything left behind there.

He did not tell his father about his suspension from the university; he was afraid of pounding the streets too much and being recognized; and he did not want to see anyone, particularly not Helen, in his present setup which was strictly an interregnum, he said to himself. Thus mornings, which he could not spend at home without explanation, he went to the public library and read popular novels. Then he went back home and sat in his room, allegedly to study.

His mother was cheered up by his return, and she announced she would soon be on her feet again.

He had been home a week when he was told at the contact address that Despard was free and living under another name somewhere in the country. A. left a letter for delivery to him.

That evening his father called him into the study with a somber face, and A. thought, damn, he has found out. But that was not it.

"An official letter came for you," his father told him. "I haven't opened it but I think I know what it is."

"Ministry of Defense" it said on the envelope. It informed him that he had to report within forty-eight hours at the National Barracks for induction into the army.

"I thought as much," his father said, "but it must be a mistake. You are a student. We don't have to worry about it; I would pay for a replacement anyway."

A. began to laugh. "You can't do that," he said, "it was one of our demands to abolish that system."

"What? Whose demands?"

"Oh, nothing," A. said hastily, "some student action. Anyway, I was suspended from the university. I didn't want to upset you, and especially not mother. But this is not a mistake, it's a punishment."

The following evening his father told him, "I don't want to know what you have been up to. You're back home and you're still my son. I was promised today that a replacement can be provided."

A. thought, I really hate myself, look at him, he is so pleased with what he has achieved for me and he thinks I'll be so grateful, the poor devil. "I'm really sorry," he said, "I'm really beholden. But I can't accept it."

His father looked at him. "You're a fool then," he finally said sharply, "as I've often suspected."

"Well, I'm the only one to suffer for it."

"I hate the idea that a son of mine would be a fool. It is natural that I take care of you if you are unable to do so yourself. Don't you realize that it is a law of nature, taking care of yourself? You've tried to go against the laws of this country, and that was bad enough. And what did it get you? You looked like a beggar when you came back. But do you now want to defy the laws of nature too? A bird, a bug, know to take care of themselves. So now you want to drill in the mud with a lot of ignorant peasants, be sent God knows where, throw away months or years of your life, perhaps your life itself?

"I thought you were such a patriot?" A. asked.

"What has that to do with it? Don't you radicals even have the instinct of self-preservation? Do you deny even that?"

L

A UNIFORM is a sacerdotal vestment, a soldier is no longer a simple human being but a priest of death.

He knew he had copied those words in a notebook once, or had he thought them up himself? He was standing in line in the unpaved courtyard of hard frozen earth, and wondered if he should refuse to accept his uniform. He looked at the shaven neck of the farmer's son in front of him. The boy turned around and whispered, "You must watch it, they always give out shoes that are too small." Then he reached the doorway of the storeroom; two men behind a counter were handing out gear. There was no officer in sight; what would they do if he refused to pick up his things? He got to the counter; the man behind it, a corporal, took a look at him and said, "We haven't got your size yet." A. began to laugh. The corporal laughed too. "That's right," he said, "we must keep our tempers, it's no use griping. Here's boots anyway."

"What should I do then?" A. asked.

"Do? Come back and try again. Half the goddamn platoon is still in civvies. Next."

So much for the priesthood of death. The wickedness and stupidity of this world is at least mitigated by inefficiency. I wonder if revolutionaries are enough aware of that. It probably works both ways. They overestimate our cleverness. Police reports like newspapers overheat reality. That will be the march of progress: the evil will remain, the inefficiency will be overcome.

He went to open a window but there were so many cries of protest that he had to close it again.

How can you get any sleep in this room with all these men snoring away at two-feet distance? You probably have to become an officer just to get a good night's sleep. I still live in a bourgeois conservative reactionary body that is perfectly willing to eat cake.

"Hey—you—what did you do before?" a neighbor asked him.

"I was a student."

"I thought so. I'm from the city too. I'm a clerk in the railway administration. Most of these boys are just peasants, they're like cattle. Did you see their feet?"

Here's where I make a little speech about solidarity for the working classes, A. thought, but he only said, "Well—"

"I've been promised an office job," the railway clerk said. "I've got a letter from my doctor about my chest."

"Listen," A. asked, "where exactly is this camp? Is it near a main line?"

"You bet it is," the clerk answered proficiently. "Didn't you hear that long whistle before? That's the night express—four hours to the capital. We're on the

southern trunk line running parallel—only freight,
timber from the mountains—if you had your own
train, say if you had a private train, like the president
does, it'd be an hour to the junction, three hours to the
city, you'd be home in bed before midnight."

LI

HE FOUND himself not refusing the uniform when it
came, and he was going through the motions like
everyone around him. It was hard to connect these
mainly good-natured, slow, boys marching and coun-
termarching around a courtyard, with the weird game
of war, the numbered ranks used up by strutting
officers male animals in death plumage, with the gov-
ernmental, official, the indeed sacerdotal killing of
other men. Killing was such a criminal word; it
seemed impossible suddenly that a government would
ever have announced, "We killed so and so many of
the enemy—", as if they would write in the paper,
"We stole so and so much money."

The discipline was supposed to be harsh; but in this
out-of-the-way camp their officers were seldom
around, and they had the luck of an old, fat sergeant,
about to be retired, who had only a few teeth left and
no interest at all any more in martialness.

A. was made a corporal because he had had an

education, and he did not protest it; it meant a better bed near the entrance of the dormitory.

In the beginning the others showed a tendency to pick on him for practical jokes, but when they saw he was just as uneager to follow the rules or get ahead as most of them, they stopped. But their defiance of authority had nothing rebellious in it and was simply based on their suspicion of another world they would never enter; and A.'s feeble attempt to instill some politics into the discussions which came up after the lights had been put out brought no reaction. They did not even talk about girls much; the only subject of general interest was food.

Rifles came, and except for the few men who had experience as hunters, they were handled with awkwardness, with inimicality almost. It was different when bayonets were issued. All of them, even the railway clerk with the weak chest, twisted these around with a certain voluptuousness in the straw hearts and livers of the old paillasses put up for that purpose. "The human body has twenty-eight feet of intestine," the old sergeant shouted at them, which created general laughter. "You just get hold of it somewhere, underneath and up, like this, like a knitting needle in your mother's wool, and you pull—and no one, not even Jesus Christ himself, can stuff it back in, the man's had it."

LII

"ALL DAY today for cleaning and pipe claying," the sergeant announced at the morning parade. "Tomorrow inspection by the captain. So get with it. Remember, any trouble I have, you have—but worse." A. waited until they had gone for their breakfasts, and went over to him. He asked if it were true that they would be posted in a little mining town nearby.

"True," the sergeant said, "though I'm not allowed to say so."

"But why would they want a garrison in such a place," A. asked, more of himself than of the old sergeant. "They must be crazy."

"Ha!" the sergeant cried, "now you're calling your superior officers crazy. Let me tell you, Corporal, they know what they're doing. Better than you or me."

"They do?"

"They do," the sergeant answered with a self-satisfied air.

A. shrugged, which annoyed the man. "You want to know why?" he added, "because there's going to be trouble in the mines. From the Reds."

"Oh," A. said.

"Now you'd better go get your breakfast."

A. came outside and slowly crossed the yard to

where the tail end of the breakfast line was disappearing into the kitchen. Day had broken, the low camp buildings were outlined against a milk-white sky. He shivered with cold, but it was the wet cold of dawn: the sun, soon to rise over the treeless hills around them, would be warm. The patches of dirty snow would get still smaller. It was spring, if the late and hesitant spring in the foothills of the southern mountains.

He hastily swallowed his corn coffee and ate his porridge; then he went to see the paymaster.

"I wonder if I can have the pay that's coming to me," he said.

"Now?" the paymaster asked horrified. "Do you know the work I have, to close out the accounts here?"

"No, but I'd like all the same—"

"Saturday," the paymaster said. "What difference does it make to you? You aren't going anywhere, are you?"

Like the others, he spent that day polishing his boots, thinning out pipe clay and sponging it on his anklets and belt, polishing his rifle. When dusk fell, he took a paper parcel he had prepared from under his bed and walked to the gate. "You have a cigaret to spare till tomorrow?" he asked the sentry. "I'll share one with you," the boy answered. He rolled two thin cigarets out of one pinch of tobacco and lit them. "It's damn cold," he said and went back into his little hut.

A. half turned, then walked on through the gate and up the country road which curved from the camp into the hills and vanished into the dark low fog banks of the evening. It was that easy. At the first cluster of trees, he took off his uniform and put on his student jacket and his trousers which he had carried in his parcel. He was tempted to put his army greatcoat back on, but decided against. He left the coat and uniform there.

Two hours later he came to the little mining town.

Intermittently, he had seen its web of lights in the distance, but when he reached it, it was lying dark and deserted. A single light was burning behind a window on the main street. He went up to it, but could see nothing through the heavy curtain. The house itself looked neutral and had no name or sign. Then that light went out, too. It was like a door shut in your face. As he stood there, the echo of his steps had died out without leaving another sound to be heard. The town had locked itself in, all its life was turned inward.

The mud under his feet felt sharp, it was freezing again. He bit his lip and sucked his breath in through his teeth. He knew he was not too far removed from a state of panic.

He walked on and at the second side street he saw the lantern of a café. He hastily went in.

There were some tables occupied by small groups of men who fell silent as he opened the door. He ordered a gin at the counter without paying attention to them, and did not turn around until the sound of voices behind his back had resumed. At one table, the men had black rings under their eyes in white faces; they were coal miners. A. waited as long as he could; but when he thought from the activities of the café owner, who was mopping up the counter and putting things away, that the place could close any moment, he went over to their table and sat down. They stared at him.

"You don't know me," A. said hastily. "But I'm a member of the, of a workers' organization in the capital. And I've come to warn you. I don't know what's happening in your town, but I know you're in trouble—I know something's going on. I've come to warn you. They're sending troops. Day after tomorrow there'll be a garrison of about a hundred men posted here."

One of the men stood up. "Let's go," he said to the others, "I don't know what this fellow's talking about."

A. had a vision of a night passed walking through the frozen silent streets of the little town.

But another man said, "He looks all right to me. You got to trust some people."

LIII

HE SLEPT that night in a miner's cottage, in a warm, soft bed alone in a room. The man who put him up said as he opened a low gate, "We must be quiet. They're all asleep"; he took A.'s arm, for it was pitch-dark, and leading him through some bushes which rustled against their legs, he added, "you can piss here." Then A. was taken to his room and the door closed behind him. He dropped his clothes on the floor and found the bed by touch. It smelled clean, of soap and ironing. Stretching out in it was a pure, sensual pleasure, and the sheet against his face felt so good that it seemed almost a pity not to stay awake a bit longer.

As he came out early the following morning, he found that his host had made up a bed for himself on a decrepit couch. In a third room the host's sister, a mine catastrophe widow, stayed with two children. They ate a big breakfast of fried potatoes with bacon rinds. "I'm embarrassed," A. said, "I didn't want you—" The host smiled upon him and upon the food. "That's how it'll be everywhere, afterward—," he announced, "you believe in brother-hood, don't you?" He said the word brotherhood as if it were a kind of brother, a monk or priest whose name was "Hood."

"Yes, I do," A. answered.

An hour later another man had taken him away from the cottage and hurried him through the fields to a freight yard; somebody, one of their own men, had denounced A. to the police and the word was out to catch him, "a deserter and labor agitator from the capital." He was wearing a miner's cap and coat, and now they were half running along an unused railway track, overgrown with high weeds. They came to a siding where several flatcars were standing, heaped with coal which was white with frost.

"Christ, do I have to hide in one of those?" A. asked.

His guide laughed. "No mate, we do better than that. You travel in a caboose. Just sit on the floor, keep your head low. The conductor is one of ours. Here's four francs we collected for you."

In the little iron room at the end of his freight car he began by crouching, for the floor was moist and very dirty, but after a long wait he gave up on that, sat down, and untangled his legs. At times there were distant steps, voices. He was not afraid, in a kind of stupor rather, with all speculation suspended. And then finally, blissfully, the train began to move. He waited a while longer and stood up to look out. They were running down a narrow valley; on both sides were pine woods with occasionally an open field. The sun had risen above the trees and only threads of morning fog were left. Ahead of him he could see nothing but the coal on the car.

He stamped his feet to get his blood running again and began, a bit idiotically he thought, to sing. Because there was such a marvelous feeling of freedom in moving, in rolling north at what seemed great speed, leaving behind him the little town which he had seen only at night and would only remember as it had appeared that evening, dark, cold, shut, the empty cobblestoned street glistening with moisture and gaps in the pavement of frozen mud, the lamp behind the window soundlessly extinguished. Blind windows, a blind street, a fitting apotheosis, he told himself, of his army camp. Done with that too; he was himself again, his own man.

For that camp, with all its chumminess, its jokes, its we're-all-regular-boys-together, everyone the same food, the same bed, the same clothes, the ease of the thoughtless life, the pleasure of air, marching, feeling your body doing its work, was but pseudo-equality, pseudo-fraternity, had still been but a blind street in an empty, shuttered town, Death, and its well-fed inhabitants but walking obedient parcels of twenty-eight feet of intestines each.

LIV

IT TOOK the freight train most of the day to reach the mainline junction—there were so many stops and maneuvers. They came to a final halt with a great deal of hissing of released steam from the engine; someone walked by and knocked three times on the door of the caboose—a signal from the conductor whom he never did see—and then all became very quiet. He looked through his little window and jumped out onto the ground.

They had descended to the lowland that day, and now, although it was almost evening, the air had a softer feeling to it. It was fresh but it had lost its inimicality. It's spring, he said to himself, thank heaven that damn winter is finally done with; the grey heaps of snow along the city sidewalks, the bitter wind in their eyes during the evening canvassings, were like symbols. All will be different now, easier.

He looked up and down the line. No one was in sight, a wooden freight station stood dark, the red sky reflected in its windows. Beyond it, a birch wood began. Far in the distance were lights, of a town perhaps, or only of some railway works. He knew he should be tired, hungry and afraid, but he did not succeed in conjuring up these emotions. He simply felt happy within his own skin, totally free and unencumbered. An empty stomach stimulates your brain, it's like being drunk.

The train personnel must have gone *somewhere* to eat and sleep—he decided to see what the lights were which were now blinking through the darkening air. After a short walk he came to another station, this one of brick, with benches and a ticket window. A double track led through it. There was no one there either. In the waiting room he found a schedule posted; two trains daily left for the capital, one at six in the morning and one at noon. He opened the door to the platform and just as he stepped out, a train thundered through the station, cutting his breath and filling up the space under the glass roof with steam and smoke. Involuntarily he jumped back, and stared. Dark freight cars, and then suddenly lit windows, tables with little lamps on them, men and women dining, reading, talking. Eyes met his, it seemed, glanced past him. It was gone, a red lamp vanished in the twilight.

LV

HE WOKE from his doze on the waiting room bench at the first light, and went outside to wash under a tap he had found the evening before. It was a bright morning. I'm stiff and sore as an old dog, and I still feel as good as yesterday, well, almost, just because with God knows how many police after me, still no one can tell me what to do.

At half past five a clerk appeared and installed himself in the ticket booth. Some farmers, heavily loaded with bundles, made a momentary line. A. went up to the window and asked the price of a third-class ticket to the capital.

"Twelve francs."

He had four. He studied the schedule which gave the distances; the capital was two hundred and twelve kilometers away. He chose the name of a town listed at sixty-six kilometers.

"Three francs ninety-five," the clerk said.

The six o'clock train was short, with wooden coaches of the most old-fashioned kind; a first-class coach at the end and four third-class ones. He boarded the last compartment in the last third-class coach. It had two wooden benches, facing each other, and it soon became crowded. There were farmers and workmen, and all carried bundles, valises, and food. As soon as the train started moving, everyone began to eat.

Nothing but moving mouths—a concert of chewing with the rattle of the wheels on the trestles as a conductor. Sausages, chunks of cheese. Bread, raining crumbs. Tomatoes, spurting little drops of juice and seeds on chins and coats. I haven't eaten since that miner's potatoes. If I stare at them long enough, someone will offer me something.

His mouth was metallically dry, he looked at each of his neighbors across from him in turn, and then at those on each side of him on his bench, counting five seconds for each stare. Like the beam of a lighthouse on a sea shore, he thought. You have to do this scientifically. No one caught his glance.

"God, I'm hungry," he suddenly said aloud, blushing at the same time and looking at his feet. I shouldn't have humiliated myself like that.

But when he looked up again, no one looked at him and they were all eating as if they had not heard.

Goddamn their souls. Goddamn the people, screw the goddamn revolution. He pulled his pen out from his pocket, the only object he carried on him, that and the five cents change from his ticket. "I have a pen here," he said to no one in particular. "Very handsome, too. It has a cap which comes off like this." He demonstrated, his eyes focused on his hands. "I forgot my provisions," he then said. "Anyone wants to swap?"

After a second, he felt a hand on his. A farmer's wife pushed half a loaf of bread and a sausage in his hand, and without waiting took the pen.

When the train stopped at his station, he descended and without standing still or checking if he was observed, got back on into the first-class compartment behind his, closed the door and crept headlong under the purple velvet bench. He pressed himself against the wall and lay motionless on his back, looking up at the springs and breathing in the dusty smell of the old velvet material.

LVI

THE TRAIN entered the capital in midafternoon. He was determined to be more clever than whoever might be after him, and after a moment's wait he got out from under his bench, dusted himself off, left the train and marched straight into the men's room on the platform, where he locked himself into a toilet. He could see the daylight over the partition, along the ceiling, and he stayed there until it was dark. Those were miserable hours. Then he came out, walked to the far end of the platform, jumped down onto the tracks and ran. All this was necessary because at that station, tickets were checked once more at the exit gate. When he saw the lamps of a street on his right, he jumped down the talus and said to himself, I made it. How have you been getting on without me in this town? I'm back. It took him a while to get oriented, then he set out for his contact address. It was a risk, but there seemed little choice.

A man whom he had never seen before opened the door. "I'm Leonard," he told A., standing a foot away from him in the narrow corridor while holding the front door open on a crack and peeking out. "I know of you, but you can't stay here. We're lying low, we're under attack, and we're penniless. I've got my instructions to use this house only in real emergencies."

"This is a real enough one," A. answered.

"I'm sure you've done fine work. But you'll agree you weren't a big man in the organization. The police aren't likely to be still looking for you. Even if they do, a few weeks—"

"A few weeks? It so happens I'd be shot. I deserted."

"Oh—" Leonard said and stared at him. "Wait here."

He walked away and closed a door behind him. A. heard the diffused murmur of voices behind it. Who's there, whom is he consulting?

Leonard came back and said solemnly, "You must stay here, for the time being. We'll wait for further instructions. Come in here." He led A. into a front room and opened a drawer. "This bottle is peroxide. We think you should use it on your hair. It'll make you look very different."

"All right."

"Perhaps you're hungry?"

A. was on the verge of answering, "No, thanks," but then thought, that would be pride carried too far. "Yes, perhaps I am," he said in an unfriendly voice.

They looked at each other.

"Do you know where Despard is?" A. asked.

"Nobody does."

Fed, washed, and with clean underclothes—strange woolen drawers with buttons, five sizes too large, from heaven knows whom—he sat in his little room and looked out of the window. It had been impressed upon

him that it was too risky to leave the house. After
some argument, Leonard had agreed to have a note of
his delivered to his mother. The message came back
that they had been worried about him and that she
was getting well. Their house was surely under sur-
veillance, Leonard said.

On the corner of the street stood a tall chestnut tree
which he could just see without opening the window.
It was covered with little pale green leaves like a veil
and he sat looking at it until the street became dark.

LVII

A meeting of a dozen men; some faces he knew, many
new ones. If only Despard were here. A man needs at
least one ally. These people are just polite, doing their
duty. They don't give a damn really.

They were discussing him.

"It's too tricky to have him stay in this house in-
definitely. It's too risky for him to work in this town."

"I've always said we shouldn't—" one man began.

"Well, there's no point in going into that now."

"My sitting in my room serves no purpose," A. said.

"What do you want to do?"

"To get back to work. That's what it was all about.
I've been away, I don't know what's going on. What
are we working on?"

A silence.

"Actually, we're not working on anything right now," the man who had been acting in charge of the proceedings answered. "No need to be embarrassed about it," he added, looking around the table. "We're under attack, we're lying low. Our only concern right now is to survive as an organization in this town."

"That's a pretty negative program," someone said.

"It's a pretty difficult program."

"Despard wouldn't—"

"But Despard isn't here," the first speaker interrupted. "We're in politics. Politics is the art of the possible."

"Then why did we try a general strike?" A. said, surprising himself. "Surely everyone knew that wasn't really possible?"

That remark created indignant shouts of "Yes, it was!"

The chairman lifted a hand. "No it was not possible," he announced. "And we knew. At least I knew. Despard knew. We went through with it all the same. Because it was needed—to show the workmen of this town, to show the people that this is still a feudal society. Feudalism not of birth but of money. Not of knights but of army men, corrupt judges, politicians, police. We needed that strike attempt to break the myth of national solidarity, and the myth of our parental government. Our government isn't parents and the country isn't family."

"And all those poor bastards in jail, and our men in hiding?"

The chairman shrugged. "The revolution—our Association is like an army. We have to take orders."

A young man wandering around aimlessly in the back whispered to A., "I don't like armies."

A. grinned. "I just ran away from one."

"Let's get out of here," the young man said.

When they were standing in the corridor, A. asked, "Who are you?"

"I live here too. I'm called Leonard II. I'm a cousin of his." He walked down the stairs and opened the front door.

"I'm not supposed to leave this house," A. said.

"You're just as safe on the street as in here, if you ask me," Leonard II said. "They talk too much."

"Perhaps you're right. I'd like a look at the sky, I must say."

Out in the street, the boy said, "I'm almost eighteen. I'm going to join the others."

A. began to laugh.

"Why does that make you laugh?" the boy asked indignantly. "Don't you know that power corrupts? Our organizers have been in charge too long."

"Are you saying they're corrupt?"

"Not like that—not that they sell themselves. Their leadership is more important for them now than the thing they lead. That's why they talk so. They don't want to take any risks. They're in love with the beauti-ful paper setup."

"Perhaps you're right," A. said, again. "Anyway, that's not why I was laughing. I used to talk about joining the others."

"Did you?"

"Yes. But you—the Association—was the others."

The boy did not understand. "The others," he said, "are the anarchists. The black flag."

A. said nothing.

"They believe in propaganda by the deed," the boy went on, "not by the word. The destructive urge is a creative urge."

"I'm sure you're quoting someone there," A. said, "someone who was sitting in a nice cozy study as he wrote that."

"Someone who had been chained to a prison wall for ten years," Leonard II said.

"Who was it?"

"Oh, never mind. I'll show you what kind of things I'm talking about. Do you want to help in a plan?"

"Yes."

"Do you know the municipal pawnshop?"

"I sure do," A. answered.

LVIII

THEY HAD called their plan "the day of the poor."
With A., they were four, among them a clerk in the
municipal pawnshop. Early one morning, Leonard II
and one of these men went to the house of the pawnshop manager. A. and Joseph, the clerk, waited at the
store. The manager lived alone; the idea was to get
hold of him just as he left his house, lock him up, and
take the key of the shop. A. had waited only a few
minutes when Leonard II appeared, walking calmly
and nodding and smiling at them from a distance. "It
worked fine," he said, "hardly a scuffle. Here's the key,
let's go in. He's in a closet, very nicely, with a chair to
sit on. Michael is sitting on the other side of the door.
His front door's locked and the blinds are drawn."

The three of them now hastily put on the lights in
the store, took the shutters down and unwrapped two
signs they had brought. These said, "On the Occasion
of the Birthday of our Beloved President, all Pledges
may be Redeemed Free of Charge." They put one in
each window with much laughter and running out
into the street to see how they looked. But it remained
quiet.

Their first customer was a young man who wanted

to redeem a violin. "Here's the money and the inter-est," he said, "ten francs fifty."

"Didn't you read the sign?"

"No, what sign? Is something wrong?"

"No, nothing is wrong. It's free today. Just take your violin. And your money."

The boy stared worriedly at them, then took the violin and left in a hurry. They could see him reading and rereading the announcements.

Next the other clerk of the shop came in. They knew what to do; Leonard posted himself at the door. "What's going on here?" the clerk cried, "Where's Mr Postum?"

A. said, "He's sick. I'm taking his place."

The clerk looked him up and down and frowned unbelievingly. "And those signs," he went on. "They make no sense. And anyway, the president's birthday is in August."

"Sit down," Joseph said, gently pushing him on both shoulders, "and listen. We've decided to give the people back what's theirs. Either you help, or we'll know how to take care of you."

"But you can't do that," the clerk protested in a whining voice, "Joseph—think of the bookkeeping, it'll be a mess."

They began to laugh.

"You must be crazy," the clerk said, "Who's behind this? Who are these fellows?"

"The people's behind this," A. answered. "We are

the people. We think it's immoral that our town earns a profit, that some bastards are making money from the misery of others. You realize that some poor slob pledges his winter coat for five francs and pays ten percent interest—" "Thirty-five percent," Joseph said. "Thirty-five percent, just enough for one shareholder in this noble institution to buy himself a cigar? Today—"

"Here's a customer coming," Leonard II said from the door.

"Quick," A. cried, and he and Joseph took the clerk by his arms and hustled him out and into the backroom. "Where can we put him?" A. asked. "In the basement, he'll be safe there," Joseph said.

"You'll be sorry for this," the clerk told them.

When they came back into the store, there were four people waiting for their possessions. And from then on, the word spread at a geometrical rate. The three of them could hardly keep up with the stream; they were running around, Joseph shouting instructions at them, while the waiting customers, mainly women and children, were buzzing with excitement. "What do we do with people bringing things?" Joseph shouted. Just give them their money," Leonard II said, "and let them keep their stuff."

He and A. stood in the doorway for a moment. A nice spectacle: a woman walking away clutching a big and very ugly lamp, looking over her shoulder as if expecting to be stopped at the last moment, another carrying a torn paper parcel of bedclothes, two children lugging a clock. "My dinner jacket," A. suddenly said. "Joseph, where are evening clothes?"

On a rack covered with brown paper hung dinner jackets and cutaways in all states of more or less faded elegance. There were also vests, capes, and even top hats; all in a cloud of camphor smell. A. found his suit and took it off the rack. A yellowed dry carnation was still sticking in the buttonhole. Imagine that, that was me buying boutonnieres. I must have had a marvelous time.

"Look at that crowd," Joseph said. "This won't work much longer." Just then they heard a door bang in the back of the house. Joseph dropped the tickets he was holding and left the room. He came back in a great hurry and told them softly, "Let's get out of here quick. He's got away. He'll bring the police." A. grabbed his dinner jacket, and Leonard II took the interest ledgers from the shelf and put them under his jacket. "We'll be back shortly," he called to the startled customers, "In the meantime, help yourself."

There was never a word about the day of the poor in the newspapers, but it made its impression. Joseph was taken in by Leonard II afterward to sleep in his room, and he told them that the event was discussed in the neighborhood with mounting excitement, "with awe almost," he said. A myth was born from that parade of women and children carrying home pots, pans, clocks, shoes, sheets. The free return of a coat or a suit or a blanket, the sudden release of their shoddy possessions from that iron grip of power and legality, assumed in retrospect a vastly exaggerated, miraculous proportion to them, seemed to turn the very laws of nature upside down. Some of them became so scared that they returned their things. The day of reckoning, the Last Judgment itself, were mentioned.

LIX

Despard reappeared out of nowhere.

Everything became different. Men who used to hold forth at great length were silent; others who had not been seen since the strike showed up. Despard did not talk about lying low; he suggested the opposite course. The more they were lying low, the easier for the police to pick them off one by one. Everyone out into the street, that was the answer. They couldn't put thousands of people in jail, at least not without crippling the town. The first of May was to be their day. They should work on this one goal, to turn out the greatest May Day demonstration ever seen.

There was nothing particularly ingenious about that plan; why did his little speech do so much to revive everyone, and clear the atmosphere of all the bickering and sullenness? Not because of what

Despard says, A. thought, but of course because of the kind of person he is. Here's certainly an uncorrupted man. He doesn't want us to follow him, he wants to be a sort of catalyst. I can listen to him and fit in, do what he wants me to do, and feel at the same time as free as that first evening of spring, at the freight station, a week ago, with no one in the whole world knowing where I was, who I was.

A policy meeting was scheduled and messages sent out, discreetly but without the precautions they had been taking lately; the place chosen was a restaurant owned by a member. A notice on its door said, "Closed for family wedding," and they were to come in in small groups at different times, but it was as near to open activity as they had been in many months. Despard gave A. a set of papers identifying him as a master printer from another town (he had brought dozens of those) and told him he could come—as long as he didn't expect to be asked for his opinion.

A. would later think of that restaurant afternoon as *the* meeting. Although nothing lasting would come from it, he would in his most somber moods feel that because of it, everything had been worth it; because of it he had, emotionally and very unsophisticatedly, known what it was all for.

The only plan discussed was Despard's May Day demonstration. Delegates from other districts and even from other towns weighed the pro and con, and the more they talked, the more a mood of excitement and lightheartedness took hold of the room. They'd had a time of terror, it was said, but the terror was in their own hearts, they had been afraid. A man shouldn't be afraid—let *them* be afraid. We'll get our men out of jail—or join them. And when finally someone wanted to put the plan to a vote, there was a general cry, "Not necessary! Yes! Yes!" and applause and cheering.

Despard was to make the last speech. "But," he said, "everything has been said. And in better words than I had prepared." He turned to sit down again, but those beside him would not let him. He made a face, got back onto the little platform and sat himself behind the old piano which stood in a corner. And with one finger, but hitting very hard on the keys, he began

They laughed, and looked at each other; one man jumped up and closed the window. They started to sing. It was a song A. had never heard, (and he was told later that none of them had ever sung it openly) and which ended, "and tomorrow, the Internationale will be the fate of man." A. was sitting halfway back in the room, against the wall, and he watched all these men sing, a hodgepodge of types. This will be my anthem, the only anthem without guns or kings or God as the commander-in-chief of our army. There were men in their Sunday best with scrubbed pink cheeks, and others unshaven and grimy, dapper young

men, bent beaten-looking men, some heavy formida-
ble women, two young girls, clean, dirty, fresh,
smelly, sweating, stupid, wise, greedy, saintly, ugly-
looking people. Nearest to him stood an old man, or
perhaps a man just looking old, with a greyish stubbly
face, a white shirt with a stained detachable collar, a
black tie in a big knot, and a black strangely cut
jacket. Tears were running down this man's face, and
as he caught A.'s eyes, he nodded as if to affirm them,
smiled at him, and said, "Yes, tomorrow."

LX

As SUDDENLY as the May Day plan had come up, as
abruptly it was scotched. Nothing more should be
aimed for than neighborhood meetings, and these only
on the Sunday after May 1—thus was the word from
"up high" as Despard put it. He appeared to take it
lightly; "they think I'm too sanguine," he repeated to
everyone, stressing the word sanguine.

On the day this news came, A. was called in and
severely rebuked for his share in the day of the poor.
Leonard announced that he did not want A. to stay in
the house unless he promised to stay off the street.

"If you lock him in," someone said, "he may as well
take himself to prison."

"It's not a matter of locking him up. It's a matter of
the way he acts; he makes risks for the others."

"It's the old beef again, you're against him because he's a student."

"I won't talk personalities," Leonard announced.

"The only point to consider is——"

Shall I tell them I don't *want* to stay? He saw himself making a short, sharp statement, something to really show up Leonard as an ass, and then get up and walk out of the room and out of the house. No, I won't. We're still one group, God, if we can't make it, if this sad little handful can't stick—I won't dig a petty personal triumph out of all this confusion.

"We all run risks. If you want to dodge risks, you should leave, not A."

Holy Joe, they're on my side against Leonard.

"A. should stay until he has a better place. And we'll trust him to be careful on his own terms. Everyone agreed?"

Now I really have to leave. But quietly, in the evening. Nothing staged.

He sat in the little room and looked at the tree. He knew what he was going to do: wait until after dark, then leave with some borrowed money in his pocket. Go toward South Hill, where else? God, saints, angels, let Helen be home. Not on a trip. Not on some damn vacation. He'd wait in a café, send her a message. He had done that before.

But precisely because he had done it before, she wouldn't come this time.

I'm sick of this after-dark routine anyway. I'm only an ex-corporal ex-student, not a famous spy.

No more messages either. I'll ring the bell. I'm still the Latin tutor, no, the dinner guest.

He combed his hair, borrowed a tie out of Leonard's closet, and left the house. The sun was shining and he walked straight up toward South Hill, smiling indiscriminately on girls, children, policemen.

LXI

As SOON as she saw him, she started to laugh. "What is it?" he asked, half-puzzled, half-offended.

"Your hair, you look so funny!" Helen cried. He had forgotten all about his peroxide hair.

The second thing she did was to ask, "Have you left it all behind you?"

Behind me—I'd forgotten how prissy she talks. She hasn't changed a bit. "I don't know," he said.

Not what I had anticipated at all. I'd expected anger and a rebuff, or a big fuss, where have you been, why didn't you even write. She's a cool girl, after all.

He had thought it wise to be vague about himself, not to worry her, but now it seemed much better to impress her instead. "I have to hide," he said, "and you're the only one, the only person in the world, who can help me."

She giggled nervously and bit on a nail. "Honestly?"

she asked. "Or is this one of those games of yours again?"

He did not answer.

She gave him a long, searching look which made him uncomfortable, and he ended it by turning his head away. He walked toward the door. Try mother next, he thought, if only she's out of bed, if I can only get hold of her without my father knowing.

Helen stopped him at the door and smiled at him, very sweetly and touchingly even, it seemed. "Come," she said.

She tiptoed through the conservatory with him and brought him out into the garden. The long shadow of the house cut it in two; it was already green, first dank, then sunny; in the back, behind a kitchen garden and a row of trees, stood a shack, built against the garden wall. It was dim inside, empty, with a vague smell of apples and potatoes. "It's not used for anything any more," she said in a low voice, "won't it make a marvelous hide-out?"

He smiled.

She held a finger against her lips. "Wait here," she whispered. "I'll be back."

He watched her dart back to the house, her legs and her hair very light and then vanishing in the dark green.

LXII

SHE CAME BACK with half a dozen blankets. "They'd just been put in the summer chest, they'll never be missed," she said, puffing and dropping them all on the floor. She brushed her hair out of her face. "My parents are going out in an hour," she added, "and then I'll bring you dinner."

She showed up with a picnic basket filled with an odd assortment of food, and they sat down on the blankets with it. "I told my mother I wasn't hungry," Helen said, "I waited to have dinner with you."

"Thank you."

"It wouldn't have been polite to let you eat alone," she said gravely. "Tell me, what would happen if you were found? What are you hiding from?"

She is acting out an idea, a story, and I shouldn't be too realistic about it; a deserted corporal has little dramatic quality.

He could not think of what to say, and ended up just smiling mysteriously.

She put her hand on his for a second. "But now you must be sensible again," she announced.

"But I'm very sensible."

She sighed and dropped a piece of chocolate she had been biting at, back into the basket. "I understand better than you give me credit for," she said. "Sunday, last Sunday, when it was so warm and springlike suddenly, I was sitting in the conservatory . . ."

Her voice trailed off. He waited.

"And it all seemed so dreary, so stultifying. So inane, as you once said. This is such a little town really. What do we all do here? Life in big towns is different, isn't it?"

A., who had never been in a big town, answered yes.

"And I understood you," Helen went on. "I wanted to run away too, to do things, change things. But all I could think of was knocking over a vase, the crystal one with the peacock feathers. And I was ashamed afterward, and I told my mother I had knocked it over by accident." She looked at him to see his reaction.

The revolution is not an antidote for bored young ladies and gentlemen.

Still—. Her words conjured up his Sunday picture again for him, again the silent Sunday streets; Sunday is reality day, without the makeup of hustling and bustling. A hundred thousand satiated, constipated, clogged-with-selfishness drawing rooms. They want and have more and more and more, but strangely there's nothing for them to hope for. No hope, no risk.

That's one of the reasons they manage to get the young men off to their wars, he then thought. It's the only excitement they have created, without a scrap of danger to property, business, or their Sunday roast.

All they expend is our eyes, legs, balls, intestines, and heads. They've understood the temptation of terror and barricades, of attack, and directed it neatly away from them. Perhaps we *can* sell revolution as an anti-dote. Use all that boredom and turn it around.

"And you know what I realized?" Helen asked. "All the novels I've read, all those that end happily— there's always a house, and a safe income, and the hero and the heroine live happily ever after, just like that, doing nothing more for the rest of their lives."

"Ye-es," A. said, "that's our dream, the empty dream. What can you expect? Money is our yardstick and so what can you ask of people once they have it? Take soup to the poor, good works. They do that."

"While in your world—?"

"In my world? In my world there'd be hope." He thought about his answer and decided he liked it. "A world without hope is just a physical world. Like an aquarium and like a terrarium. Like an army camp. Like the world of army officers. Animals live in a world without hope. But innocently. We've got neither hope nor innocence."

"Were you in the army?" she asked.

"Yes."

"And you ran away?"

"Not exactly. I had a job to do, I had to go warn friends."

"Couldn't you have gone back afterwards, and just told them that you had been on a spree?"

He looked at her with some astonishment.

"A cousin of mine did that," she explained. "There was a party he didn't want to miss. Everyone knew about it. They locked him up, but only for a week."

"I didn't want to go back, we were going to garrison a strike town."

"But now, if they ever find you, they'd—they'd—" She turned pale and did not finish the sentence.

"You make me feel very dramatic," he said, "though I know I'm not."

LXIII

HE SAT on his blankets in the doorway of the shack. Helen had pointed out her window to him, on the second floor, under the mansard, at the corner of the house. As it grew dark, lights went on all over the house, then, one by one, they went out again. A light on the ground floor remained, barely visible through the trees, her father's study; and the light in her bedroom. It grew cold and he draped some blankets over his shoulders.

He could not make himself go in. It was too pleasing to be sitting in her garden, huddled, and look at the steady light from her room which filled him with an unknown feeling of peace.

It was a kind of looking up at an imagined castle, and it seemed weird that this girl ate at one table with, touched, kissed, a man like her father; that she was nothing more than a daughter in a household like any other. He thought that sleeping with her, literally, lying in one bed with her through a night, would be a greater intrusion, a greater breaching of walls, than making love. Then again it was nothing like that, it was just a game; she had transformed this hiding of his into a children's game. He had never had that kind of childhood with brothers and sisters, gardens, tree houses; now suddenly he had a younger sister and they were acting robbers or Indians. It is a bit too soft and too childish, another temptation she offers unknowingly.

The light in her bedroom went out, on again, out, on and out. He laughed. It must have been meant as a good night greeting to him. Of course she knew I was watching her window, that would be part of her libretto. He went in, closed the door, took off his shoes, and rolled himself in the blankets.

Lying there on the floor, after a while he could distinguish the dim grey square of the shack window in the blackness. There were little sounds all around him, workings in the wood, rats or squirrels or whatever lived there. When he held his breath, he could hear the rustle of the tree tops in the wind. Some insect or other creature walked across his hand. The warmth of his body in all those blankets enveloped him and made him tingle. His thoughts grew vague. He fell asleep to the soft sound of his mother's voice downstairs.

LXIV

UNDER THE FERNS and the potted palms of the green-house, his chair pulled up as closely as possible to the glass, he watched the garden lying in the rain, streaks of water running down the panes, a soft ticking every-where, the path outside along the wall filling with puddles in which brown leaves of last year were floating around. He was left there by Helen, with the *Illustration* from Paris and the Italian magazines, a cover with a man on a camel attacked by a panther, the man with bulging eyes, purple blood running down the camel's side. A greater reality than a photo-graph, the reality of horror in the mind of the man who drew it. It sickened him and he got up and threw the magazine behind a cabinet.

Helen came in, wet and very young-looking, in a raincoat and a rain hat. She shook herself. "My mother will be here after dinner," she said quickly. "She knows you're here."

"I've been afraid of that. Did she tell your father yet?"

"I promised her you'd leave tomorrow. That was her condition for not giving us away."

"Oh." He had meant to move on, but it was a bit disconcerting, this calm way in which she had dis-posed of him.

"I have to run upstairs," Helen said, "I'm soaked. Don't move. I have to tell you something."

He could hear her steps on the staircase. What a strange girl, what a strange time he had spent here. A little theater play. Her good deed. What did I make up, what was real?

The rain changed to a heavy downpour, and for a moment it was almost dark in the conservatory; a false light reflected from the sky into the puddles; the drops struck so hard that each made a bubble on the ground. There was a rumble of thunder far away. God, I feel sad. I'm going to lie low, Leonard's favorite expression. Where? Perhaps in my father's attic, ask him would he please get me in the clear, and I'll sign and promise anything and take my punishment.

A shiver went through him; Helen had come back in without him hearing her steps, and put her hand on his shoulder.

"Did you hear the thunder?" she asked. "That was the final farewell of winter."

She bent over him and looked at him. "Did you know that's what it means?" she insisted.

"No," he finally answered.

"You know," Helen said, "I'm going with you tomorrow."

"What!" he shouted.

"Ssh."

"Oh no, you're not," he said. He felt embarrassed

now by his own behavior. Here I was sulking and feeling treated badly. She must have seen it. What an ass I am. She didn't ask me to desert. Why am I always fishing for appreciation. What a chance I missed there to act like a man.

He jumped up and took her hands. "You are a marvelous girl," he said softly. "You make me feel a million pounds lighter. But you're staying right here. That's the end of the little story. Being on the run is not funny at all, not like a romance."

"You know me very little," she answered. "I'm coming with you."

She turned on a light, and they looked at their reflection in the dark glass streaming with rain.

LXV

THEY SETTLED for a compromise plan, mainly hers, and she took him to her parents' summer house ten miles from town, by a long ride on a streetcar and then a walk down a country lane from the last stop. While in public she held on to his arm or his hand and made them look very unsuspiciously like a young couple on an outing. As soon as they were out of everyone's sight, on a gravel road descending through the fields, she let go of his arm and put her hands in the pockets of her raincoat.

The house, shuttered and musty, stood beside a greenish little pond. She ran around opening all the windows. "There're no neighbors," she told him, "no one can see you. The only building is next to us, and it's empty. There used to be a pottery in it."

That was a low brick structure, surrounded by a crumbling wall. They walked up to it through the high grass which was still wet from the rains of the day before, and looked at it. "Give me a push," she asked, "I want to sit on top."

They sat on the wall, keeping their eyes half closed and lifting their faces to the sun which was in and out; holding hands and very still.

"I have to go back," she said. "Will you be all right here?"

He nodded.

"There's lots of things in the cellar, you'll see. Even wine. You must be careful with fire. Will you be lonely?"

"Yes."

"It's just for a while, till they've stopped watching for you. You can sleep in my room if you want to. I'll show you."

"You shouldn't do all this. Your parents will be furious."

"I don't care if they are. I want to live my own life. I'll be back soon. You must let me help you, I can take messages from town back and forth for you."

"It's not so simple," A. said.

"All those Russian girls did it. Did you ever read about them, those students, like the girl who shot the police chief of St. Petersburg? Some of them were hanged."

"Yes I know," he said somberly.

"And they were so pretty."

She came back two days later and found him very dirty and unshaven in the kitchen, cooking potatoes. "I couldn't get the pump to work," he told her, "I haven't washed since you left."

"I'll show you how," Helen said. "And I've brought you bread, and a lot of newspapers. But you look well. The country becomes you."

He made a grimace. "I've been lying in the sun mostly. There's really nothing to do here. I must get back to town."

"What about my father's library?" she asked.

"It's all collected works in leather bindings of men I have managed to avoid so far. I refuse to read authors with long middle names."

She came again a day later and told him she had been to the Leonard house, and that the word was for him to stay put. "I can't," A. said, "this is really not what it was all for. I am going back with you, if you'll let me. We look very innocent together."

"And once you're in town?"

"I don't know yet, I'll improvise."

"I thought you'd say that," Helen said, "and I won't let you. They say it's crazy, an unwarranted risk."

"Oh for godssake," A. said, " 'unwarranted.' Unwarranted indeed."

She looked at him and walked out into the garden.

LXVI

HE COULD see her from the kitchen through the half-circle window which was just above ground level; she was leaning over the wall with her back toward the house. She did not stir and he went out after her.

When he was standing beside her, she kept staring at the empty pottery factory. "I'm sorry," he said. Now she looked at him, with tears in her eyes. "It's just that it seems so idiotic for you to get yourself killed," she said. "But if that's what you've set your mind on— And I know 'unwarranted' is a pompous word."

"Oh—" he began, and did not know what else to say.

"Will you stay if I stay too?" she asked.

"You stay? And what about your parents, then?"

"I left a letter this morning. It's all right."

"But how could you know?" he asked.

She was pleased. "You think I'm a schoolgirl. I'll surprise you yet."

It has become a green and luminous day, green and

luminous, green and luminous; and we're not very much acting like those brave girl students, more like the persons in a Russian novel, one of those summer country-house stories of total indulging in emotions, with me the well-meaning somewhat corpulent country doctor and Helen the frustrated young genteel but impoverished governess. Or better, me the eager, poor student and Helen the confused beautiful heiress to the estate. I should feel guilty. It's nice to let yourself drift and you can even find the consolation in it of saying, now it's all my fault, not the world's. I'd rather accuse myself than the world. It must happen so often like this, not really a girl and an empty house with trees and a pond of course, but their equivalents. And the people are thus always and inevitably let down. Even the word "people" has been spoiled by us for them, it smells of phony political speeches; but they're always ready and always better than anyone could hope or expect them to be, and they're always let down and nothing changes. Well, I'll think about it later.

The afternoon sun had reached the open space between the trees and the pottery and shone into the house, surprisingly lighting up the darkest corners of the room. "I've found candles," Helen said. "You shouldn't have been sitting in the dark here those evenings."

Then the sun went behind the building and it became quickly dark around them. They had been reading, each in a corner of the couch, and now they just sat there. They put their books down and nobody said anything or moved, and Helen did not light the candle she had brought.

LXVII

" 'We want to have morality instead of egoism, honesty before honor, principles instead of usage, duty instead of decorum, reason rather than fashion, hatred of vice rather than hatred of misery, pride instead of insolence, love of fame rather than love of money, merit instead of intrigue, truth instead of cleverness, good people instead of good company, the greatness of man instead of the pettiness of great men . . .' " He asked her, "Do you know who wrote that?"

"And listen to this, 'On the thirteenth of Ventôse of the year Two, Saint-Just said, Happiness is a new idea in Europe.' "

The year Two.

In November 1793, the French Assembly decided to adopt a new calendar. The equinox of the previous autumn, September 22, 1792, the day on which the constitution had been voted, was declared the first day of the year One.

The nerve. What unfathomable exhilaration must have possessed these men to do such a thing.

You have to assume then that they really believed that everything was going to be *that* different, that the world had entered a totally new time. I wonder if that can ever happen again, anywhere, if ever again a body of people will get together on this earth, so completely without cynicism or disillusion that they want to start with day one, year one.

"It was abandoned again, obviously," he told her. "That's never specified; I looked it up. It was quite a while later, actually, when Napoleon had already been emperor for more than a year. They must long have been afraid to. Can you see how they must have felt? I'm sure they had all sorts of explanations, it wasn't practical, the rest of the world, etcetera—and yet—it was such a dreary move. Of course everybody knew things were long back to normal and that the whole sensible-fraud, the Christian dog eats Christian dog circus, was once more in force. But when the new calendar was thrown out, and the old tired years were back, it sealed it, or so it would have seemed. All for nought."

"It sounds a bit unreal to me," she said, "and old-fashioned. I thought your people talked about surplus value and things like that."

"Surplus value?"

She laughed. "I've been reading things too."

"Oh," he answered. "I guess they do—but clever

governments and clever owners get to that, too; what they call enlightened self-interest. Can you think of a more gruesome expression? Equity isn't the antidote to the humiliation of man, fraternity is. . . . Or I could just tell you, never mind socialism, let's be aesthetic, once we had knights and they're beautiful; the men in power now are so terribly ugly, their power is ugly; and men on barricades are beautiful again."

LXVIII

BEYOND the pottery building, the road dwindled and continued as a footpath, with on its right pine trees and on the left a plowed field of brown earth in which sand glistened. Where the field ended, trees grew on both sides, but farther and farther apart, with bare little hills covered with dry grass, bushes and heather. The ground was very uneven here and it was not easy to walk. Then the terrain descended and they came upon a narrow stream.

"My feet hurt," Helen said, "I'm going to dip them in the water."

"It looks sort of slimy."

"I don't mind. They're algae, they're clean. You must look the other way a minute."

He let himself fall back on the grass.

Over his head, clouds were blown across the sky at

great speed, one moment it was all unbroken white, then there were great loopholes of pale blue; out of the corner of his eye he saw Helen roll down her stockings, smooth her skirt, and then take the stockings off. She was much too neat and decisive in all her movements to give it any sex connotation; it doesn't even fit that she told me to look away. You could almost think she was flirting, telling me that. But she isn't, of course, she is indeed the most sisterly creature I've ever laid eyes on. He sat up and watched her feet, she was kicking away the green on the surface of the water and holding them just barely under. He lay down, stretched, and let himself roll toward her. She dipped her hand in the stream and then put it on his forehead.

"Oh I like that," he said closing his eyes.

And he saw Anne, he saw her nude belly as if it were the mouth of a fish opening and closing and blowing bubbles. What an insane thought, where did it come from? The body of a girl.

Helen's legs; if I'd put out an arm, I could put my hand against her bare leg. I'd love to do that. Now I've done it, I've de-sisterized her.

"May I use your handkerchief to dry my feet?" she asked.

"I haven't got a handkerchief. You can use my sweater."

She laughed. "You know what," she said, "if, ten years from now, we come to this house and remember—" "Ten years from now!" he interrupted her. She blushed fleetingly and did not finish her sentence.

He looked at her. "Do you remember the first time you saw me?" he asked her.

"Yes, of course, when you came to teach me Latin and our maid—"

"No, before then."

She considered and shook her head. "When?"

"No, never mind."

"Please tell me," she said.

"Some day. Some long winter evening."

"Do you promise?"

"Yes."

After a while she asked, "Have you often done that? Follow girls, accost them, get to know them that way?"

"No, certainly not," he said, "never! What do you think of me? And that never works anyway."

"Well, it worked with me."

He was surprised. "Well—yes," he said. "But that was different."

They walked back to the house very slowly, shuffling their feet through the grass. She had agreed to have a look in town with him the following day, and the idea hung over them and made them hold on to their time. Once in the house, the day would be over. I'm crazy, he thought, why can't I just *be*. By common accord they did not go in but turned and walked around the pottery. They peeked in the windows, and he tried the doors but they were locked.

With a sigh, he put his arm around her shoulder, and they entered the house.

LXIX

THE STREETCAR tracks ran through a country lane first, on the left side of the road, past villas, rows of poplars, walls, pastures; then they entered the outskirts of the town where cottages and semidetached houses mixed town and country life, the worst of both worlds, he thought. Names of the houses, Mon Repos, Amilda, changed to numbers. A stop in a square, and then they were in the real town, surrounded by stone, and the towers and churches seen in glimpses of the river and the river quay. They came to the terminal. "Last stop," the conductor called when they didn't get up. "Come on," Helen said.

Making their way through a crowded street. They had never really been in this town together. "I hope we won't meet someone I know," Helen said, keeping her head down.

"They won't recognize you with that kerchief around your head."

"Where will you wait?" she asked.

"Nowhere. I want to come too and talk to Despard

myself if he's there. No one is on the lookout for me any more, I don't think."

Despard had grown a beard and looked very strange. The three of them were sitting around a wooden table with a velvet tablecloth in one of the rooms of the Leonard house.

He had expected that Helen would have felt her duty done when she had piloted him safely through the town, but she went into the house with him and sat down so matter-of-factly that it would have been awkward to send her away. "I'm A.'s friend," she said to Despard, who seemed to think it quite natural too.

It was a depressing conversation. Despard has changed, not just that beard, he's so lifeless.

"Yes," Despard said as if answering A.'s thoughts, "we're suffering from a degree of paralysis."

"But *why?*"

"For one thing, we have word to await the outcome of the trial, the court-martial I mean."

Under the "militarization of factories" order, a number of strikers in the capital and other places were on trial as deserters.

"There's a friend of yours among them," Despard told him with a wry smile. "That man who put you up your first night when you had come from the army camp to warn them."

A. was startled. "That's terrible," he said, "how do you know?"

"We're in contact. They smuggle letters out."

"But what are you doing about it?"

"Nothing. What can we do?" Despard answered. And he repeated, looking at Helen this time, "Nothing. We used to throw smoke bombs, as he knows"— he nodded in A.'s direction—"but we've outgrown that."

No one spoke.

"You must excuse me," Despard said, "I have to do some things. Just sit here, they'll bring you something to eat."

When they were alone, A. rested his head on his hand.

"You mustn't be too disappointed," he said to Helen. "I know this is not the way you'd expect things to be. Me neither. It's hard to explain . . . from a distance, when you're sort of floating above it all, it seems so simple, just a matter of being determined. I remember how I felt standing on that bridge in the rain, last November . . . but then the closer you are, the more complicated it is. You get lost in details. Despard really is a marvelous man . . . I'm disappointed too—"

She smiled reassuringly at him. "But I'm not disappointed," she said. "You mustn't expect too much of people. They get tired."

A child came in, after knocking on the door, took off the tablecloth and folded it up and put a plate of sandwiches on the table. Then Despard returned, more cheerful. "I've managed a room for you two," he said, "if you have really decided not to leave town, that is." He waited a moment, and when they did not speak, went on, "You'll be safe there, anyway. But you must be quiet, and no light. Just a candle on the floor perhaps."

A. looked at Helen but she seemed quite unconcerned. "It's on the top floor of an old office building," Despard said. "Some archives or other. The watchman is completely reliable."

LXX

IT WAS more than just an old office building, it was a sixteenth-century palace, run down and apparently about to collapse, but with dramatic, curved steps and stone lions and heralds, housing the municipal archives. A burly man with a faded military decoration on his jacket led them up a back staircase and showed them to a little room, with only an iron bedstead and a table with a pitcher of water.

"You can hang that there, I guess," he told A. in a doubtful voice. He was referring to the dinner jacket which A. for reasons unknown to himself had brought with him from the Leonard house, and which clearly bewildered the watchman. He pointed out a candle. "We've electric light here," he said, "but you mustn't use it, it shows from the street. In fact, if you don't mind, madam," he said to Helen, "I better take the bulb out. Avoids a mistake, you see."

"I don't mind," Helen said laughingly.

When he had closed the door behind him, she sat down with a bounce on the bed. A cloud of dust rose. Then she became serious and looked somewhat guiltily at A. "I know it's not a game," she said, "but you must admit, it's sort of dramatic, this room."

He smiled at her. "Yes, sort of," he answered. "You're starting to talk like me."

"We'd better go to sleep," she said.

"Yes, but—I'll sleep on the floor," he announced.

"No you don't have to do that. I trust you, you're my brother."

He made a face. "Well, not really, you know," he said.

She half closed her eyes and nodded.

They kept all their clothes on and lay beside each other under the thin bedspread, very chastely, and she suddenly whispered in his ear, "I love you too." Then she turned over and did not move any more, and he could hear from her breathing that she had immediately fallen asleep.

A vague and diffused light entered the room. He lay still, afraid to wake her, and stared up at the ceiling in which some long-dead sculptor had fashioned a garland of roses with a cupid in the middle, who knows with what expectations, what pleasurable ideas?

It was quiet but for the occasional rattle of a passing carriage.

Then a soft ticking began; it was raining. He very carefully got up and looked out of the window. The street below was glistening already, empty, and beyond the corner he could see the river, just a gleam, and the soft circles of light around the lamps on the embankment. He felt filled with love, for everyone, for everything; for this town, and for mankind, he thought.

He lay down again and very gently pulled up the bedspread. He turned his face toward her and touched her hair with his mouth.

LXXI

THE WATCHMAN knocked and put his head around the door. Helen opened her eyes and said sleepily, "Yes?" A. awoke, saw that it was day, saw the watchman's face, and thought, here we go, they've come to get me. He jumped out of bed and as he sat on the floor to put on his shoes, he found that he was not afraid, simply very alert, trying to remember the structure of the building and asking himself if it were feasible to get away through the window and across the roof. He stood up and looked at the watchman, waiting for the word, but the man just smiled, looking much more friendly than the night before, and said, "There's coffee and bread in the basement, in my apartment."

A. laughed at himself. When you're really in for it, you never expect it. And the other way around, perhaps.

The watchman's head disappeared, he was waiting for them in the corridor. Helen rubbed her eyes and got up too, her hair tousled and with a childish fold in her face where she had slept on her hand. "Good morning sister," he said.

Later she took a note of his to Leonard II, who promptly came to see him in their room in the archives building. They talked about the court-martial of the strikers.

Something would be done.

In the middle of the afternoon, a young woman showed up and said she would take A. to meet a friend. She looked very manly and efficient; she was a nurse, she told them. Helen wanted to come too, and the three of them left the crumbling palace out of a courtyard door, after squeezing their way through a corridor filled with piles of folders, smelling of dust and dried and breaking papers.

It had stopped raining, but the sky, and the river under it, were grey. "It's a day when nature can be of no help to man," the nurse said. And added, "I read those words somewhere and I've always remembered them."

"They're quite striking," Helen answered.

The two women started talking and were soon deep in conversation; A., not saying anything, walked in between them, but half a step behind, every now and again turning his face toward each of them.

He tried to swallow away the rising tension in him.

LXXII

THEY CAME to a district where he had never been. The street ended at a little round bridge, too narrow for wheeled traffic, spanning a canal. Across that bridge, to the right, stood a long brick building reaching right to the edge of the water, and beside it, in the open air under a corrugated iron roof, a loud, shaky steam engine was running. To the left of the bridge was a scurvy grass field full of bare patches.

Streams of green, yellow, and orange liquid ran from pipes piercing the wall out into the canal, as if the building were exuding poison.

The nurse walked ahead of them to the steam-engine shack. As they followed her, Helen opened a little iron door in the side wall of the main building and looked in. Rows of women and girls were at work, seated at tables in a dark hall, lit only by a dismal light coming in through window panes around the wall below the roof. The draft rattled the door but

they did not look up. Helen stood still and stared,
until A. closed the door and pulled her away.

"This is my fiancé," the nurse shouted over the din
of the steam engine, and presented a somber young
man in oil-stained overalls. "He's the mechanic."

There were handshakes and nods all around.

"This is a fine place to talk," the mechanic shouted,
"they can't overhear us. So you're willing to come in
on this?"

A. nodded. "We must all think up something, but
there's no time to lose," he said. The nurse and her
young man nodded in turn. Helen, who had tears in
her eyes from the steam, the wind, or the noise, was
obviously determined to be as tough as everyone else.
A. could hear her say, "Yes."

Then she took a step forward and said to the
mechanic, "I'm available too, for whatever you think I
can do."

"We've got pyroxyline here, heaps of it," the
mechanic shouted with a triumphant air.

"Oh," A. answered, and "Oh," Helen said.

I forgot what that is, if I ever knew. Perhaps an
explosive. Poor, sweet Helen, sagely nodding her
head once more, happy too that we have pyroxyline
although she cannot have the slightest notion what it
is. This is a terrible place to decide to love her, a
sulphur-laden wind howling around us, our feet on
cold mud and our heads in hot steam, everything
shaking and clanking and banging, the sixth circle of

hell, and as a moat the poisoned green and yellow waters, made bitter by the burning fire falling upon the third part of the rivers and the fountains; this tender soft girl, and me too, lost among a starched nurse with big no-nonsense hands and her puritanical fiancé who has clearly never yet shown need to put his hand on one of her breasts or behold the softness of the skin of her thighs; what are we doing here? But no Helen I mustn't weaken.

LXXIII

THE MECHANIC had brought a stepladder and was tinkering with the lamp in one of the new ornamental lampposts that flanked the Military Building.

A. sat on a stone bench reading *The People*. Facing him, fifteen feet below, lay the square in front of the building; stone steps led from it to the front entrance, and where he sat a grass-covered little park sloped down to the square. It was young spring grass and two fences, above and below, were to stop children from running or in winter, sledding, down it. The mild morning sun was shining. He had told Helen he was visiting his mother. It would have been impossible to involve her in this.

On his level, a street led to the side entrance of the building and then around it. The door on his side, fifty feet to the right of the bench and looked down on by the mechanic from his ladder, was the door the presiding judge of the court-martial would come out of, as he did every day. The trial would be finished before noon. A girl with a brown hat, whom A. had not met, would follow the judge out.

There were only two things the judge, an army colonel, could do: release the strikers, or have them shot. If he had ordered them released, the girl would come out with the hat in her hand and wave it. If the judge had condemned these men to death, she would wear her hat.

The judge, coming out that day followed by a girl wearing a brown hat who would then step back into the building, would have condemned himself to death too, for the mechanic would throw a bomb at him from his ladder. If the mechanic missed or his device failed to go off, A. was to throw his, which he was holding in his lap under *The People*. There were no specific plans for after that. The colonel always went to his luncheon club alone. If, unforeseen, he had someone with him, the brown-hat girl was to improvise something to detain his companion.

It was indeed quite simple.

A.'s bomb did not look in the least the way he had imagined a bomb; it was a metal soldered box. It isn't round and it isn't ticking the way they do in magazine stories. My lunch sandwiches could be in it. Well, it's a bit heavy for that. One of my mother's not quite succeeded cakes.

That thought seemed very funny to him.

How did I ever get to this point, and to this stone bench, and with this box? All I set out to do was join the Radical committee, in order to worry less about injustice, to sleep a bit better you might almost say. Do I want to kill this man, is it right, does it serve a purpose; I think it does, but I do not know if the purpose is worth it.

The black flag. Propaganda by the deed. The externalization of idealism, the only impeccably logical consequence of freedom, and justice.

I hope the girl will wave her hat. Let's say the chances are fifty-fifty. And then, if she doesn't, chances are let us say ninety to ten that the mechanic who was going to kill this colonel anyway, will do so. Which leaves a five per cent chance that I will have to put my paper down and throw this idiotic box at a man I've never seen before.

I'm not afraid and I wonder why. Perhaps because this isn't me doing this, it's an abstraction of justice. Godhelpme, it is history. I'm not afraid from lack of thought but from too much. But it would be miserable to die at this age, not to know what will happen afterward, not to know ever. Vanish tracelessly. The perpetual sunlight, the perpetual silence, of the universe.

Vanish tracelessly.

What will Helen say? How will she look, will I be there, will I be gone? Will she one future night lie in a bed, with a man on her body, some man who will have her, who will feel the pressure of his own hand, through her body, on himself, while I will have ceased to exist? Would she think of me, re-create me? I wish she was like those Russian girls, I wish she was sitting here beside me. I'd be totally satisfied with everything then.

How much the *now* seems all—always, to every one of us, of course. A good thought that. Think of Stendhal, the world for him was a world melancholy for Napoleon, that one flicker of time was what he knew, what he imagined it was all about. Or some young man living under Caesar, their ups and downs was *it* to him, the gist, the core, the facts of life. And here I am and I imagine that nothing has ever existed but that oak door, this little street with houses on one side and the park down to the square on the other, a fellow on a ladder, me on a bench, and a colonel and a girl in a brown hat. But it is nothing, well almost nothing, and people will sit here, or on a bench like it, for generations and centuries afterward unaware of *my* now, of this newspaper, of this little editorial column with its signature and line of little dots, this date at the top of the page, this fold in the paper, the weight of this iron box on my leg, my left shoelace which broke this morning and has a knot in it.

But since happiness is nothing too, since the grass where I sat with Helen and the iron bedstead in the archives palace are just as forgettable, and after us no one will ever know how we felt . . . nor will they know about anything else, that early evening on a field, some school thing, when the sky rose so quickly that I thought I was pulled up into it, or once the street with the music from an open window. The music hoping for everything. . . . This way I have at least in some lopsided way done something about my marvelous bridge dream, about that morning looking down upon the river, and the tugboat, and my leg which had just mended, the black water, the drizzle on my face. The towers and the churches through the rain. Judica me Deus et discerne causam meam de gente non sancta.

I hope that girl comes out with her hat off.

A NOTE ABOUT THE AUTHOR

HANS KONINGSBERGER was born in Amsterdam, Holland and studied at the University of Zurich, but all his published works, beginning with his first novel, *The Affair*, were written originally in English. During the Second World War, he was in the underground and later reached England where he served in the British Army; he has been writing in English ever since. In 1951 he arrived in the United States on a freighter from Singapore, and made his home in New York.

His previous novels, *The Affair, An American Romance, A Walk with Love and Death*, and *I Know What I'm Doing*, have met with considerable critical acclaim here, and they have been widely translated and published abroad. In 1965 he was the first America-based novelist in many years to visit China. The outcome of this journey was the book *Love and Hate in China*, most of which was first published in *The New Yorker*.

His play *Hermione* was performed in Europe in 1964. He has written for newspapers and magazines, including *The New York Times, The Nation, Saturday Review, The New Yorker, Guardian*, and *Punch*.